SNAP

CAROL SNOW

An Imprint of HarperCollins*Publishers*

For Lucy, who loves taking pictures;
and for Philip, who loves to be in them.

HarperTeen is an imprint of HarperCollins Publishers.

Snap
Copyright © 2009 by Carol Snow
All rights reserved. Printed in the United States of America.
No part of this book may be used or reproduced in any manner whatsoever
without written permission except in the case of brief quotations embodied in critical
articles and reviews. For information address HarperCollins Children's Books,
a division of HarperCollins Publishers, 10 East 53rd Street,
New York, NY 10022.
www.harperteen.com

Library of Congress Cataloging-in-Publication Data
Snow, Carol.
  Snap / by Carol Snow. — 1st ed.
    p. cm.
  Summary: When fifteen-year-old Madison's parents, who are having problems, bring
her to a seedy beachside town, she relies on some quirky new friends for help figuring
out how her camera is taking pictures of people who are not there, and who later suffer
tragedies.
  ISBN 978-0-06-145211-6 (trade bdg.)
  [1. Supernatural—Fiction. 2. Photography—Fiction. 3. Cameras—Fiction. 4. Family
problems—Fiction. 5. Friendship—Fiction. 6. Beaches—Fiction.] I. Title.
PZ7.S6807Sn 2009   2009014581
[Fic]—dc22   CIP
                                                                             AC

Typography by Michelle Gengaro-Kokmen
09 10 11 12 13   LP/RRDB   10 9 8 7 6 5 4 3 2 1
❖
First Edition

I.

IT WASN'T EVEN A VERY GOOD PHOTOGRAPH.

The lighting was lame, for one thing. Midday light is never ideal, but the problem wasn't the overhead glare; it was the fog that choked the beach with a heavy whiteness. There were no shadows, no depth—nothing but a bleached-out deadness.

And then there was the problem of a focal point. There wasn't one. A row of boulders rose on one side. Next to some concrete steps a sign said KEEP OFF ROCKS. A sandy stretch, narrow in the foreground, widened to a fuzzy beach beyond, the distant people looking like dim dots, not the splashes of color I'd envisioned. There was the ocean, of course, a dull stretch so colorless that you could only guess at the line that separated water from horizon.

Finally, there was the old woman standing next to the rocks, completely ruining whatever beauty the scene had to offer. In a bathrobe and slippers, she didn't add to the beach vibe at all. Plus, she was looking at the camera, at me, as if I'd interrupted her somehow, as if it weren't the other way around.

No, it wasn't a very good photograph. I would have deleted it from my camera without a thought, except for one thing.

When I took the photograph, the old woman wasn't there.

2.

BEFORE I CAME TO SANDYLAND, freaky stuff like this didn't happen. If my pictures looked different than reality, it was because I'd experimented with the camera's settings or messed around on the computer.

Before I came to Sandyland, life made sense.

We weren't even supposed to be here. Our original family plans—"family" meaning me and my parents—called for a cruise around Hawaii, where I'd photograph fire dancers and sunsets and turtles instead of creepy old ladies skulking around in the fog.

Hawaii! Four islands in eighteen days! And my parents cancelled the trip! Okay, I know that sounds totally spoiled, like "Poor me, getting cheated out of two and a half weeks on a cruise ship," but vacations were what my parents and I did together. They were our bonding time. In previous summers we had forged stronger family ties in Bermuda, Mexico, and the south of France. The rest of the year we just kind of lived our separate lives in the same general vicinity.

The crazy thing is, I was psyched about Sandyland. Originally my dad was going to come alone. Some guy he knew found him a couple of weeks' work in town—nothing great, just some construction gig—and he was going to crash at a cheap hotel. My dad's a building contractor—he specializes in custom homes—and ever since the economy tanked, his business had been less than fabulous. "Money is tight" had become my mother's mantra, followed closely by, "You don't know how good you have it."

That's when she said anything at all. My family was never exactly what you'd call chatty, but lately the usual silences had been joined by hostile glares (from my mother) and apologetic throat clearing (from my father). My reaction was to stay in my room as much as possible and try not to think about it.

But my dad's work had always come in spurts. Something would turn up. Then my mom would take me to the mall for some desperately needed new clothes, give me some spending money, and reinstate my cancelled cell phone service. (That? Really bummed me out.)

When I told my best friend, Lexie Larstrom, that my dad was going away to work for a few weeks, she gave me this really odd look.

So I said, "What?"

And she said, "Don't you think it's weird—that your dad would go to the beach and leave you and your mom here?" Lexie's family has a lake house, and her dad would never go there alone.

So I started thinking. Is this some kind of trial separation? Am I about to become a Child of Divorce? Will I have to stand up in court and say which of my parents I love more? Will they make me go to a counselor so I can talk about my feelings?

Then, on Thursday night, my mom had come into my room and said, "So that beach town—you know, we said Dad would go alone, but we're going to go with him. So you should pack. We leave Saturday. Dad starts work Monday."

She didn't smile, but then my mom's not exactly a smiley sort, so I just felt relieved because I wouldn't have to go to a counselor and talk about my feelings. Plus, I was glad to be going somewhere—anywhere—even if it wasn't Hawaii (sniff), because our town, Amerige, gets really hot in the summer, and Lexie kept going off to the lake and leaving me bored and alone.

It didn't even cross my mind that summer in Sandyland might be worse than summer in Amerige. It certainly didn't occur to me that my life was about to be turned upside down.

I had just finished my freshman year at Amerige High School, where I was pulling straight A's in the honors program. (Well, okay, almost-straight A's. Let's not talk about Advanced Algebra II.) At the end of the school year, Melissa Raffman, the editor-in-chief of the school newspaper, *The Buzz*, had picked me to be a staff photographer. *The Buzz* had its own office and budget, along with a reputation for attracting the best students and the most prestigious awards. Practically everyone wanted to work on *The Buzz* because it would look so good on a college application (not that I'd ever be so calculating, ahem).

I had friends. I had my own bathroom, my own flat-screen TV, an iMac. I had a swimming pool—just a basic one, without any waterslides or caves like the Larstroms', but better than nothing. I had good hair: thick and brown, cut on an angle, ending between my shoulder blades.

Things weren't perfect, of course. My love life was in the

crapper ever since Rolf Reinhardt, my first almost-boyfriend, had publicly dumped me for the bloodsucking Celia Weaver. (On the bright side, I'd beaten Celia out for the newspaper photographer position.) By summer, the only guy who was paying any attention to me at all was pale-faced pothead Kyle Ziegenfuss, whom I'd tutored in my school's peer leadership program.

But still. Things were pretty good, all things considered.

On the day we left, my mother woke me up early—at, like, nine—handed me a cereal bar, and told me to "get moving." I threw my camera, iPod, and wallet into a beach bag and staggered out of the house. I'd packed everything else the night before, using the opportunity to sort through my summer clothes, most of which were too small, too faded, or otherwise too sucky.

As we whizzed along the freeway, my father behind the wheel of his "baby," a black Cadillac Escalade, I had no bigger concerns than:

"Does the hotel have a pool?" (No.)

"Is it on the beach?" (No.)

"Can we stop at Starbucks?" (No response.)

The drive would take us two, maybe three, hours. Sandyland was a nice place, my parents promised: small, pretty, quiet. The hotel was on the road to the beach. I'd like it there. That's what they kept saying. "It's nice. Just wait. You'll like it."

I should have known it was going to suck.

3.

"Nice" is not how I would characterize Home Suite Home. And let's just say that "hotel" was a bit of a stretch, too. If I had to pick one word to describe it, I'd go with "craptacular." I didn't say that, though, because whenever I complain about anything, my mother says, "You expect everything to be handed to you on a silver platter"—which is actually pretty funny when you consider that my mother, who's really into decorating, once collected silver platters, back in her Victorian phase.

So instead I just said, "Well, this is, uh . . ."

My mother finished the sentence for me: "Hideous."

I laughed. I thought she'd laugh, too, and we'd have this nice little mother-daughter snark-fest, but instead she just wrinkled her nose and headed for the bathroom.

The motel room—oh, sorry, "suite"—was dark: brown carpeting, brown couch, brown bedspread, heavy drapes. The space was long and narrow, with only a tiny frosted window by the front door and a sliding glass door at the far end, past the brown kitchenette.

Also, it smelled—something musty and dirty that I couldn't place. Against the wall, a brown laminate desk had a sign propped up: PETS STAY FREE! That was it: the room smelled like dogs.

Once we'd brought in all of our stuff, I asked, "Wanna hit the beach?" (Nicer, I thought, than saying, "Let's not spend one second longer than necessary in this smelly crap-hole.")

My mother said no because she had to go to the grocery store, and my father said no because—well, he didn't say anything, actually; he just lay down on the (brown) bed and turned on the (bulky, outdated) television.

I didn't bother to change out of the clothes I'd thrown on that morning: black shorts, a tight black-and-pink-striped T-shirt, and orange flip-flops. My hair was looking kind of greasy, but it wasn't like I was going to run into anyone I knew. I slung my camera case over my shoulder and made like a tree.

As advertised, the beach was right down the street. Unfortunately, the street was a mile and a half long. First I had to walk past the highway off-ramp (conveniently located right next to the motel), a McDonald's, a strip mall, and a run-down minimart. Things got nicer once I reached the middle school and town pool. Finally I hit the main drag. There were cute little pastel-colored buildings with awnings: restaurants with adorable names like Burrito Bandito and Priscilla's Pancake House and shops selling T-shirts, towels, boogie boards, and plastic sand toys.

Between a fudge shop (sorry, *shoppe*) and an antiques store, a surf shop had some really cute orange board shorts in the window. Across the street was a place called Psychic Photo. Seriously—I checked twice. It could have been worse: at first I thought it said Psycho Photo. The awning was black with silver moons and stars. The storefront was purple.

At the end of the street I glimpsed blue and kept walking until I hit the wide public beach. The air by the water was cooler than I expected, almost damp. The sky had a slight gray cast: a fog was rolling in.

I dropped my orange flip-flops into my beach bag and stepped onto the coarse sand. It felt warm and soothing on my soft feet. Not as warm and soothing as Hawaiian sand, but nice. Around me brightly colored beach umbrellas sprang from the sand like lollipops. Small children in flowered bathing suits played at the water's edge, digging and hopping and yelping. In the water, older kids rode to shore clutching boogie boards.

This was approaching acceptable.

I pulled my camera out of its black canvas case. It was a tidy silver Canon that fit snugly in my pocket or comfortably in my hand. The square screen that covered most of the back was big enough to hold my world: to scan and edit it, to zoom in close or veer far away. With a push of one button, I could freeze time. With another, I could erase an unwanted moment.

I took some pictures of the umbrellas, and then I trudged across the sand to the ocean. Small waves broke near the shore, sending icy water to bite my toes. A strand of seaweed coiled itself around my ankle like a snake. I kicked it off.

Beyond the breakers, two large birds perched atop a yellow swim float. Pelicans? Herons? Maybe they were just seagulls. I held up my camera and zoomed in—just as a couple of kids reached the float and scared the birds away. I released the shutter anyway.

(Time: 3:34 P.M. Picture quality: pathetic.)

The rhythmic whooshing of the waves soothed me. I took a deep breath and held the salty air in my lungs. It was cold and clean and tangy. It felt so good that I breathed in even deeper the next time, until I felt almost drunk with oxygen. Maybe this vacation wouldn't be so bad.

After taking a few (mediocre) shots of breaking waves, I strolled down the sand. I felt stupid in my dark clothing and wished I'd changed—not that any of the other clothes I'd packed were so great. The beach grew narrow. A rock seawall rose on the land side, a bunch of big houses above it. One had a second-story addition being built. Another had been torn down to make way for a whole new house.

I took shots of the rocks and of the concrete stairs leading to the houses. I was getting into position to snap a seagull standing on a KEEP OFF ROCKS sign when something pierced my foot. I stumbled forward. The camera flew out of my hand as if in slow motion and landed on the sand with a sickening plop. I lunged toward it, wincing in pain (I'd stepped on a shell). I hardly dared to breathe. Once I'd blown sand from the crevices around the lens, I took a deep breath, pushed the picture button, and checked the screen.

Nothing.

I hit the power button to see if the lens would retract. Nothing.

Forget the sweet air, the soft breeze, and the waterbirds. This vacation was going to suck.

A bell jangled when I opened Psychic Photo's purple door. There was another customer in the small shop already: a woman in a

10

straw visor stood in front of the digital photo printer, squinting at the screen.

Despite the funky name the store looked pretty much like a normal photo place: a display case full of cameras, racks of film, color-drenched pictures on the walls. But the walls were the same purple as the outside, and the sides of the service counter were encrusted with rhinestones, bottle caps, and shells. To my disappointment, there were no crystal balls or tarot cards.

A tall, angular girl stood behind the counter. She had the oddest hair I'd ever seen: straight and just past her shoulders, it was brown with black, blond, and pink—yes, pink—stripes. It made the unwashed mess on my head look normal.

She nodded hello.

I shot her a half smile in return.

"Don't say it," she said.

"Excuse me?" Did she expect me to comment on her hair? I wasn't that rude.

"You know." She sighed and closed her eyes. Her eyelashes were pale, as was her skin. A spray of freckles ran over the bridge of her nose. She had no curves and she wore no makeup. If not for the crazy hair, I would have guessed she was an extremely tall twelve-year-old.

Behind me, the bell jangled again, and a man walked in. He was middle-aged, with a round, squishy belly and a yellow shirt that said FISHERMEN MAKE A GREAT CATCH.

He grinned at the girl behind the counter. "I'd tell you what I'm here for, but I guess you already know."

She kept her face expressionless. "Can I help you?"

"I have film to drop off."

11

She picked up a pen and pulled a yellow envelope from behind the counter. "Your name?"

The smile was back, bigger this time. "Don't you know it already?"

She gave him a look.

"Well? Aren't you psychic?"

She tapped her pen on the counter. She had silver rings on all of her fingers, even the thumbs. "Rose will be doing readings this afternoon. She has a few openings if you'd like to make an appointment."

"Nah—just the pictures." He handed her the film.

She slipped it into a yellow envelope. "Your prints will be ready tomorrow afternoon."

His eyebrows shot up. "But the sign outside said this was a one-hour photo."

She shrugged. "The psychic is one hour. Photos take a day."

That confused him enough to shut him up.

"You waiting to download photos?" she asked me after the man left.

I shook my head. "Do you do repairs? I dropped my camera in the sand." My palms were sweating at the very thought of handing over my Canon.

At the digital printer, the woman hit a button and muttered something. On the screen two kids stood like soldiers in front of the ocean. She zoomed in, zoomed out, zoomed in again.

"Our repairman is out at sea," the girl told me, as if that made perfect sense. "He can look at it first thing tomorrow, though."

"Tomorrow's okay, I guess." I put my camera on the counter.

The woman at the printer sighed in frustration. "If I give you my memory chip, can you just print the pictures?"

"Sure," the girl said. "You can pick them up at . . ." She checked the clock behind her. "Five o'clock."

Once the woman left, I asked, "So for digital shots, this really is a one-hour photo?"

The girl smiled. Her teeth were very white, her eyeteeth slightly crooked. "It's a one-hour photo for everything. Unless you make psychic jokes. Then it takes longer."

She was definitely older than twelve.

"But you're not the psychic?" I asked carefully.

"Our in-house intuitive is Rose. She does her readings in the back room."

"Well, that's cool," I said, not knowing what else to say.

The girl retrieved a clear plastic bag, dropped my camera inside, and zipped it closed. "You got a number I can call when this is ready?"

"I'll stop by on my way to the beach tomorrow," I said, eyes on my imprisoned camera.

"'Kay." She clicked her pen. "Name?"

"Madison Sabatini." I spelled my last name for her because people always get it wrong.

"See you tomorrow, Madison."

My day almost got even crappier when I walked out to the sidewalk. A guy on a skateboard was heading straight at me and would have run me down if he hadn't managed to jump off at the last minute. He stumbled briefly before regaining his balance. I dodged out of the way of his unmanned board, which continued to whiz down the sidewalk.

I froze, heart racing, breathing heavily, and looked at the

13

skater boy. He stared back, as if he were utterly astonished to see someone coming out of a shop on Main Street in the middle of the day. His eyes were a startling green.

"Sorry," he said finally.

"You should get your board," I said.

He nodded once and then sprinted down the street.

This town was frickin' bizarre.

When I got back to "the resort" (ha, ha, ha) my dad was still lying on the bed watching some history thing on television. This was a pretty familiar way to find him—except back at home, he was usually in his double-wide chair in the den (a room that my mother insisted we call "The Library"). He was really making the most of our beach vacation.

My mother, meanwhile, was trying to figure out how to boil water. No, seriously. She was in the kitchenette (otherwise known as "two burners and a microwave") peering into a tiny pot as if it held the secret of life.

"What are you doing?" I asked, not sure I wanted to know.

"Making macaroni and cheese."

I could not have been more surprised if she'd said, "Mapping the human genome." My mother did *not* cook. Cooking was messy. Cooking took time away from hanging curtains and arranging throw pillows and watching HGTV. At home, cooking might scratch our stainless steel appliances. And on vacation? Hello?

"Aren't we going out to dinner soon anyway?" It was almost five o'clock.

She shook her head. "Not tonight."

A night stuck in one room with my parents? I tried not to groan. I failed.

My next super-special surprise came when I tried to unpack.

"Hey, Dad—where'd you put my suitcase?"

No response.

"Dad? My suitcase?"

Still lying on the brown bed, he turned his head and blinked. "What does it look like?"

"It looks like a suitcase," I said. "You know—square, canvas, has a handle? And inside? It's got these fabric things called *clothes*!"

"Don't talk to your father like that," my mother snapped. (She talked to him like that all the time.)

"Isn't it in the room?" my father asked.

"If it was in the room, don't you think she would have seen it?" my mother snarled. (See?)

My suitcase was not in the room. And it was not in the car. After some discussion, we all agreed it was right where I'd left it, in the hallway outside my bedroom at home. Instead my father had packed the shopping bag full of my old, outgrown clothes that I'd left in the kitchen, ready for my mother to drop at the Salvation Army store.

I panicked for just a moment before realizing what an opportunity this was.

"I passed a surf shop downtown today—they had some cute bathing suits in the window."

When my mother didn't respond, I plowed forward. "We can go there tomorrow. Or maybe there's a mall nearby."

My mother still didn't say anything. I took that as a yes.

15

4.

BODY SNATCHERS.

That's what I thought when I woke up the next morning and saw my mother bustling in the kitchenette—again. Was there no bagel store in this town? No Starbucks? Who was that woman handling unprocessed food?

"Did you make breakfast?" I croaked from the couch, straightening my dad's extra-large T-shirt that I'd worn as pajamas.

"There's cereal in the cabinet. Milk in the fridge."

Okay, it was still my mother.

I'd hardly gotten any sleep the night before. My father snored, my mother mumbled, and the pullout couch had spiky springs that jabbed through the thin, dusty, substandard bit of foam that passed for a mattress. In the early hours I'd finally folded the "bed" (I use the term loosely) back into the couch and slept on the scratchy cushions. Now my neck hurt from lying in an awkward position and my head buzzed from insufficient sleep.

* * *

16

We walked to the beach instead of taking the Escalade because "it's just a short walk" (not), "we could use the exercise" (speak for yourself), and "it costs ten bucks to park" (which my mother regularly spent on decorating magazines without a thought). Dressed in my black shorts and pink-and-black-striped T-shirt, I carried my beach bag and boogie board, while my mom slung her purse and a bag full of towels over her shoulder. My dad hauled the rest: a hard-sided cooler, three folding chairs, a beach umbrella, and a plastic sack full of books, magazines, sunscreen, and assorted heavy stuff. He didn't complain, but his face turned red, and sweat soaked his T-shirt in a not-so-attractive way.

They say that couples start to look alike as time goes on. Or maybe that's people and their pets. But what's weird about my parents is that the older they got, the more different they became. In our house in Amerige a framed snapshot hung in the upstairs hallway. Taken a month after they'd started dating, it showed my parents sitting on a couch holding hands, their heads tilted together. They both had thick, dark hair feathering out from their faces and thick, dark eyebrows on top of wide, happy eyes. I could barely recognize either of them. My mom had gone blond so long ago, I couldn't remember her any other way, and her eyebrows had been waxed into perfect crescents and dyed to match her hair. I called them her "Golden Arches." My dad's hair was half gray, half dark, as if it couldn't decide which way it wanted to go.

Their differences weren't just about hair. My mother got thinner as she got older. She was skinnier than I was (which was actually kind of annoying). My dad, on the other hand, looked like he had eaten too many fast-food lunches on his construction sites. Which he had. Even his face was fat. Friendly rays fanned out from his eyes, though; I liked that. My mother had a line between her Golden Arches that got deeper whenever something annoyed her.

When we reached Restaurant Row (that's a joke; there were only, like, three places), I asked, "So, where are we going for dinner tonight?"

Just thinking about food makes me happy. At that moment I was having a pretty intense fantasy about nachos.

"I've already bought hot dogs," my mother said, the line between her eyebrows deepening ever so slightly.

"Oh." She was kidding, right? I shifted my load. The boogie board was getting pretty heavy. "It's not like we have to go someplace expensive. We can just get burritos or something."

The line between my mother's eyebrows got even deeper, which meant she wasn't kidding. My father didn't say anything, just stood there oozing sweat.

That did it. "This vacation blows!" I dropped the boogie board on the sidewalk and threw my beach bag on top of it, almost tripping a little kid who was walking by. "Why are we even here if we're not going to do anything? We should've just stayed home!"

I swallowed hard to keep from crying. I'd save that for when my mother lectured me on how spoiled I was and how we all had to make sacrifices and how most fifteen-year-olds would kill to be able to spend this much time at the beach, blah, blah, blah.

But she didn't lecture me. Instead, she bent over to retrieve my beach bag and slung it over her free shoulder. Then she handed the boogie board to my dad, who somehow managed to loop the cord around the beach chairs.

We continued grimly down the street, heads bent, mouths turned down. I felt kind of embarrassed about making a scene, but this whole vacation was such a bust. I would have been okay with staying home. At least then I would have had a pool plus my own TV, a computer, and a real bed. Sleep deprivation makes me cranky. Also, if we'd stayed home I'd have my clothes. Was I really supposed to spend a day on the beach without a bathing suit?

And my parents were acting so weird—I mean, even weirder than usual. As we approached the Shopping District (photo shop, liquor store, T-shirt emporium, surf shop), I shuddered with fear—of what, I didn't know.

I stopped in front of the surf shop.

"You want to go in?" my mother said, finally.

I nodded and pushed open the door. The store was dark and cool, crowded with swimsuits, rash guard shirts, sunglasses, shell jewelry, and flip-flops. Immediately I felt better.

Like food, shopping makes me happy. The orange board shorts that I'd admired the day before didn't come in my size, but there was a super-cute bikini, white with green and orange swirls, and coordinating board shorts that had a green diagonal stripe across the front. The shorts were just the tiniest bit loose, which was good because I could eat a double cheeseburger on the beach without having to loosen them.

"Okay, then!" I chirped, coming out of the dressing room and handing the stuff to my mom. "That was easy!" I'd needed a new suit, anyway; the ones I had at home were all stretched out.

On her way to the front of the shop, my mother pulled at the price tags. Steps away from the cash register, she stopped dead. "Did you see how much these cost?"

"No," I answered honestly.

"Do you have a sale rack?" she asked the skinny girl in a

turquoise tank top who slouched on a stool behind the counter. The girl was a couple of years older than me, with a pierced eyebrow and lip.

The girl shook her head.

"Is there a Target in town?" my mother asked the girl. "Or a Wal-Mart?" (Wal-Mart? Hello?)

The girl shook her head again. "They're, like, forty minutes away." Her lip ring quivered.

"Can you give us directions?"

"Mom! I love these!" My voice cracked.

She turned to face me. "It's a hundred and thirty dollars for these three pieces."

"So?" It was my parents' fault I was at the beach without a bathing suit.

From the doorway, my father spoke. "Just get the suit. It's fine."

"It is not fine! It is—"

"Just get the damn suit!"

So I got the bikini. And the board shorts. That should have made me happy. Instead, all I could think about was the way my father had yelled at my mother. She snapped at him all the time, but he never talked to her like that. Never.

The clerk rang up the purchase as if nothing had happened—which for her, I guess, nothing had.

This was not turning out to be one of our better family-bonding trips.

Psychic Photo was across the street.

"I need to check on my camera." I kept my eyes on the ground. "You don't have to come in."

There was a green bench right outside the shop, but my parents stayed standing, weighed down by all of the beach crap and—what? Frustration? Guilt?

Walking into Psychic Photo, I felt the strangest sense of peace and relief, which I attributed to getting away from my parents. The tall girl with the striped hair, in an orange smock over jeans, stood by a photo album display talking to another girl—well, a woman—in cutoff white shorts and a tight black tank top. The woman's long, reddish brown hair was pinned haphazardly on her head, little wisps spilling around her face. Her pale gray eyes were almost freakishly huge in her thin face, giving her a hungry look. She looked around twenty-five, maybe a little younger. They had to be sisters.

The tall girl gave me a half wave. "Hey. I was just about to go check on your camera." She widened her light eyes as if in a trance and fluttered her hands in front of her face. "I must be psychic."

The auburn-haired woman in the tight tank top scowled. "Not funny."

"This is my mother, Rose," the tall girl told me. "She's doing readings today, in case you want to find out if you were, like, a cat in a former life."

It took all of my willpower not to scream, *"That's your mother?"* Instead, I just stared like a dork.

Rose thought I was reacting to the cat thing. "I don't do past-life regressions—not enough training. And I don't believe in inter-species reincarnation, as Delilah well knows." She shot a quick, annoyed glance at the girl—Delilah—before continuing. "But the energies are exceptionally strong today—the full moon

21

and the season—so if you have any chakras that you think might be blocked or if you have any unresolved issues that are manifesting themselves in . . ."

I don't know what else she said. I was too busy adding and subtracting in my head. Say Delilah is sixteen, and her mother was twenty when she had her. That would make her . . . thirty-six? Not a chance.

Okay. Say Delilah is fourteen, and her mother gave birth at eighteen. That would put Rose at thirty-two: still too old. But maybe Delilah is an especially tall and precocious ten-year-old and Rose became a mother at fifteen. Wait, that's my age!

". . . so any minute now," Delilah said, strolling over to the counter.

"Huh?" I had no idea what she had been saying.

"He's actually a fisherman," she said.

"Who?" Maybe my chakras really did need unblocking.

"Larry. The guy who does our repairs. He's in the back room, finishing work on your camera right now."

"Have you gone in the back room today, Dee?" Rose said, her voice suddenly trembling. "Did you feel the energy?"

Delilah's pale eyelashes fluttered with irritation. "I'm not psychic, Mom."

"You don't have to be." She looked at me with her huge gray eyes. There were funny shapes in the irises, like snow-flakes. "Did Dee tell you about my work with transformational experiences?"

I shook my head. Delilah and I hadn't covered transformational experiences in our previous ninety-second conversation.

"We all see the world differently, through our personal filters,"

Rose explained. "Just like a camera—you change the filter over your lens, you change what you see, right?"

I nodded. Now she was getting somewhere. I'd been saving money for a camera: one of the complicated ones with lenses you could change for distance shots. My parents had said they'd pay half. It would be less portable than my little Canon, but the picture quality would be better. I could take it to the choir concerts, the school plays, the sporting events—all the stuff I'd be covering for *The Buzz*. Now that everyone was going to be seeing my photographs, they had to be good. I hadn't given much thought to filters, which were tinted glass disks that screwed onto the lens. I'd have to look into it.

"Most people's filters are dirty or cloudy," Rose continued. "So they see the world as dirty or cloudy—and even worse they see *themselves* as dirty or cloudy."

"You can't see yourself through your own camera," Delilah muttered. (Actually, my camera has a feature where you can pull the viewing screen to the side and take a self-portrait, but I didn't say anything.)

Delilah settled herself on a stool behind the counter, which, I noticed for the first time, was covered with all kinds of—there is no nice way to say this—crap: bottle caps, straws, broken shells, pop tabs, a big wooden plank.

"So what I'm doing," Rose said, ignoring Delilah, "is helping people change their filters and see the possibilities for a new life."

"You mean like therapy?" I asked.

"God, no!" Her face twisted in disgust. "Therapy is all about, like, talking and antidepressants. A transformational experience

23

is about *energy*. When a person undergoes a transformation, it changes them forever—they actually release their old energy and become a *different person*." Maybe it was just the light, but the snowflakes in her eyes appeared to be dancing.

Delilah cleared her throat. "I'll see how Larry's doing."

I remembered that my parents were still waiting out front, so I stuck my head out of the door. "This is going to take a few more minutes," I told them. "You guys can head down to the beach— I'll meet you."

I offered to carry some of the heavy stuff, but they said they could handle it. I shrugged and went back inside to meet Larry.

He looked nothing like a camera repairman. He didn't look like a fisherman, either. He wore a black Harley-Davidson T-shirt, with a blue bandanna tied around his head. He had dark stubble on his chin, heavy eyebrows, and a cross dangling from one ear. Only his puppy-dog brown eyes saved him from mad-biker scariness.

"You the girl who's been playing catch with her camera?" He held up my Canon and scowled.

I flushed with embarrassment. "Actually, I was just taking some pictures, and I stepped on a shell. I usually leave the strap around my wrist—I don't know what happened. I guess it slipped, and—"

When I realized he was laughing, I shut up.

"Larry!" Rose scolded.

He winked at her. I'd never actually seen anyone wink without looking dorky, but Larry pulled it off. Rose jabbed him playfully on her way to the back.

At the door, she turned to face me. "What was your name again?"

24

"Madison."

She nodded as if I'd given her the right answer, tilted her head to one side, and chewed on her lip. Her unlined skin was the same translucent shade as her daughter's, her nose sprinkled with freckles. "I have a feeling we'll be seeing more of you," she said.

Once Rose had gone, Larry handed me the little silver camera, which felt lighter than usual and oddly warm, as if it had been baking in the sun. "You got lucky," he told me. "Just needed to be cleaned."

I pushed the power button, and the screen blinked to life with a reassuring chime.

"Like magic," I said.

"Nope—not magic at all." Larry pointed to the little screen, which showed my mom pruning a rosebush in front of our house in Amerige. We used to have gardeners, but my parents fired them to save money. Now half of our yard was overgrown and the other half was more or less dead. The roses looked good, though.

Larry's fingers were square at the edges, his nails cut very short. "You know how digital cameras work?"

I shook my head. As much as I loved photography, I'd never thought much about the technical stuff.

"You got your lens here," Larry said, pointing to the front of the camera. "The lens sees the light from an image—just like the lens in your eye. Inside your camera, there's a chip made out of silicon covered with millions of these tiny dots called pixels."

Larry took the camera from my hand. "When you take a picture, the pixels get all excited, and they change the energy from the light wave into photoelectrons."

I smiled politely. This was kind of boring, and I really wanted to get to the beach.

The camera flashed in my face, and I yelped.

"Sorry," Larry said, handing back my camera. "Didn't mean to scare you."

"It's okay." My heart raced. On the camera's screen I looked pale and lost, like a ghost of my usual self. *Delete*.

"After you take a picture, the camera stores the electrical charge," Larry said. "Then it converts the charge into a num-ber—you know, a digit."

When I didn't say anything, Delilah said, "As in 'digital pho-tography.'"

"Oh!" I said. "Got it." I imagined a billion tiny pixels in my head, all lighting up at once.

After Larry returned to the back of the shop, Delilah pulled a yellow slip of paper from underneath the counter and put it next to the junk.

She punched a couple of buttons on the cash register. "That'll be . . . fifty-three dollars even."

I stared at her, horrified. With all the family drama, I'd forgot-ten that I'd need money for the repair. What was I thinking, send-ing my parents away? Not that I loved the idea of asking them to pay for anything right now. My wallet was back in the room. How much was in there?

"I don't have the money," I said, finally. "At least not with me."

Deflated and embarrassed, I put the camera on the counter, next to a mound of Snapple caps. "I'll come back later." I swal-lowed hard, but the taste of misery remained. Maybe my parents and I could split the cost of the repair.

"How long are you going to be in town?" she asked.

"A couple of weeks." God, that sounded like a long time.

She studied me. "Just take it," she said after a long pause. "You can pay me next time you're downtown."

Was she serious? I checked her face. She was.

"Thanks." I tried to smile.

The beach was colder and foggier than the day before, though the fog did little to muffle the sounds of rushing waves, boat engines, and screaming seagulls. Pounding hammers echoed from a beach-front condo renovation. Camp kids in matching red bathing suits crowded the sand and water. The fog blurred their edges. They looked like something out of a dream.

It was too cold to swim, but following my surf shop victory, I had no choice but to put on my new bikini and board shorts. Once I'd returned from the restroom (which smelled like raw sewage and had no soap in the dispensers), I dropped the surf shop bag stuffed with my dark clothes on the sand next to my parents, who huddled in their beach chairs, towels over their laps, glaring at the water. Talk about negative energy.

"I'm going to take some pictures." I took a small step away before adding casually, "My camera cost fifty-three bucks to fix."

A seagull landed by my mother's feet. She shooed it away. "What's your point?" she asked finally.

I fiddled with my camera. "I didn't have any money with me. But they said I could come back later. . . ."

"And you expect us to pay for the camera that you broke." The crease between her eyebrows was huge. Next to her my father closed his eyes.

"I didn't say that." So much for their paying half. "But I might need to borrow some money. I'll pay you back when we go home in a couple of weeks."

"We might not be going home then," she told the ocean.

"Excuse me?"

"Your father—the job here . . . he's going to see if he can stay on a little longer."

I tensed. "How much longer? 'Cuz I've got that photography class the second week of August, plus Lexie is coming back from the lake. And also, Melissa—you know, *The Buzz* editor—she talked about having everyone over for a barbecue sometime this summer, and—"

"Not everything is about you, Madison," my mother interrupted, her lips turning an angry white.

"I didn't say it was." My hands shook.

"You think I'm happy?" she said. "You think I want to be here? Right now we're just trying to *survive*."

I blinked in astonishment. "Survive? You're sitting on the beach!" I was going to say more, but a group of kids walked by. I looked at the sand.

"We have no money," my mother snarled once the kids had passed. *"Don't you understand how bad things are?"*

"Stop!" my father pleaded, finally opening his eyes.

"No, *you* stop!" she said, turning her anger to him.

"Both of you stop!" I yelled—even though my father had said only, like, twenty words in the past six months. And then I turned and ran away because, frankly, I'd had enough.

Maybe divorce isn't such a bad idea after all, I thought, a sob catching in my throat the instant the words formed in my brain.

28

5.

WHAT SUCKS ABOUT HAVING A BLOWOUT FIGHT with your parents on a supposed vacation is that you can't lock yourself in your room or storm off to your best friend's house. Once I reached the parking lot, I hung a left on the sandy street that ran parallel to the water until I reached another parking lot . . . and entered a different section of the beach. Oh, yeah, I am such a badass.

Fog hovered over the sand, thick and eerie. I shot some pictures of the kids in the red bathing suits, but I was so upset that it felt like someone else was pushing the button. Still, I kept snapping because it gave me something to do.

At the beginning of the rock retaining wall, I snapped a picture of a green metal railing. I captured a waterbird dancing at the ocean's edge. Back on the public beach, the kids in red bathing suits looked like an army of ghosts. I zoomed in and took a few shots.

As I trudged along the sand next to the rocks, icy water nipped at my feet. I barely felt it. The camera remained firmly strapped to my wrist: I hadn't even paid for this repair yet; I certainly couldn't afford another one.

The sand stopped at a rock outcropping, waves slamming into the side with a slap and a whoosh. The wide public beach seemed very far away, the kids in red a fuzzy blur, the long narrow strip of beach between us deserted. It looked like the end of the world. I could almost imagine what it would feel like to be the last person on earth. If I screamed or laughed or cried, no one would hear me. I had never felt so alone.

I held up my camera and held it steady. It warmed my hands. I looked at the empty beach, made small and safe within my camera's screen, and I squeezed.

I sat on the rocks for a while, ignoring the signs that warned me to stay off, almost hoping for a rogue wave to wash me away. Not likely: the surf was pretty tame.

Once I got too cold, I headed back to the main beach and my parents, who looked both relieved and mad when they spotted me.

"Can I have the room key?" I mumbled.

"We were just about to head back," my mother said, pushing herself up from her canvas chair and sticking some things in the beach bag.

The three of us packed everything without looking at one another and trudged back to the room in silence. When we got to our door, my mother dug through her purse until she found the key.

She said, "Your father has to make a quick trip to Amerige next week. He'll bring back your suitcase."

My father put his hand on my shoulder and kept it there until I looked at him.

"I'm sorry," he whispered.

I nodded. There was really nothing else to say.

For dinner that night, my mother made blackened hot dogs. "Blackened" sounds better than "burnt," which is what they really were. The ketchup was store-brand. Store-brand ketchup is crap. I could live with Target clothes (actually, some of them are pretty cute), cheap makeup, and my mother's cooking. But asking me to give up Heinz? That was crossing the line.

We didn't talk much at dinner, which was nothing unusual since at home we normally ate in separate rooms: my mom in the kitchen, my dad in the den (oh, sorry—The Library), and me in my room with my friendly computer. It seemed weird, though, to be in one room (my mom at the table, my dad on the bed, me on the couch) and say nothing more than:

"Is there mustard?" (Dad)

"No." (Mom) And then to me, after a really, really, really long silence: "I'm going to get a job here. Just so you know."

After dinner, I took a shower, which turned out to be a surprisingly stressful experience. As I washed my hair with what I swear was bug-spray-scented shampoo, someone in another room flushed a toilet, and the spray scalded my back. I spent the rest of the shower adjusting and readjusting the temperature and pressing myself as close to the tile wall and out of the spray as possible.

I want to go home, I kept thinking. *Please let me go home.*

How much longer did my parents plan on staying? They'd never answered the question. If my mom was really going to get a job—I'd believe it when I saw it—we'd be stuck here for at least a month. Who would hire her for less than that? School started at the beginning of September, in . . . let's see . . . fifty-four days. At least we'd be home by then. (Things had to be bad if I was counting the days till I started tenth grade.) Surely they'd give me at least a week (two weeks, two and a half?) to do stuff at home before I went back to school.

Next, wearing one of my dad's big T-shirts, which was orange and said DENNIS'S BUILDING SUPPLY, I took my camera and a blanket outside. Beyond the sliding glass door, a long line of small concrete pads stretched along the length of the building, each patio "furnished" with two white plastic chairs and a matching plastic table, most of which were draped with beach towels and wet bathing suits. Beyond, a steep dirt hill speckled with scruffy grass blocked the freeway. Car fumes lay heavy in the air. I envied the cars whizzing by on the other side of the dirt divide. If only I could drive away from here.

I wrapped the blanket around myself, settled onto a slightly damp plastic chair, and turned on my camera, which glowed like a miniature movie screen in my hands. The camera was filled with shots from Amerige: the peer leadership group eating dinner at The Cheesecake Factory; a pack of friends laughing at the school lunch tables, a night at the movies. I was in a few of the shots, smiling along with everybody. That world seemed so far away.

There were a bunch of pictures taken on the day before we'd left, when I'd gone swimming with the Larstrom girls. Lexie, Brooke, and Kenzie all had long blond hair that turned white in the summer, little blue eyes, pointy noses, and slim, wiry bodies. They looked like the same person at different ages. My coloring was the exact opposite: brown hair, brown eyes, lightly tanned skin. I looked like Lexie's negative.

There was Brooke jumping into the pool. There were Lexie's long toes, the nails painted to look like ladybugs.

Oh, well. Even if I were home now, I couldn't hang out with Lexie; her family had gone to their lake house yesterday.

Next, I zipped to the shots I'd taken today. In the distance, thunder rumbled. I pulled the blanket tighter around me.

The beach shots weren't very good. Sometimes photographs look better than life. Sometimes life looks better than photographs. The kids in red had appeared so ethereal through the fog, like figures in an impressionistic painting. In the photos, they just looked blurry.

The fog didn't do much for other pictures I'd taken, either, of rails and steps and birds. All it did was block the sun and make everything look flat and dull.

And then I got to the last shot, the one I'd taken looking back from the rock outcropping.

The scene looked just like I remembered: a narrow strip of sand bordered by the rock wall, stretching through the fog until it reached the fuzzy public beach and the tiny dots of people.

Only one thing was different. There was an old woman standing next to the KEEP OFF ROCKS sign. And she was looking right at me.

6.

WHEN SOMETHING DOESN'T FIT INTO YOUR idea of the way things work, you come up with an explanation. Like:

I was distracted, so I just didn't notice the woman standing there. During the beach walk I'd been really upset, and everyone knows that the mind can play tricks.

But I was emotional; I wasn't blind. Not only was the woman close—maybe ten feet away—she was dressed weirdly for the beach, in a pink bathrobe and dirty white slippers. Her skin was almost yellow, and she was so thin that her cheeks were sunken. Only her hair looked good: bright white, full and curly, like it had just been set. There was no way I could have missed her. No way.

So I moved on to rational explanation number two.

Someone else took the picture. My mother borrowed my camera sometimes (she'd finally stopped asking me where to put the film). Maybe one of my parents took the picture when I was in the beach restroom.

Only one small problem with this theory: when I'd been in the restroom, my camera had been right with me, in the beach bag. Besides, I remembered taking that very shot, and I was positive I'd been alone.

That left me with one final, slightly puzzling but still rational explanation.

Something happened during the repair. By this I meant something technical—or, more specifically, something technical that I didn't understand. I'd always assumed double exposures only happened with film, but maybe it was possible for a digital camera to take one picture on top of another. What was it Larry had said about energy and electrons and digits?

I'd never seen the woman in the pink bathrobe, but maybe she was in the photo shop during the repair, and the camera went off, and the memory card got jumbled. Or something.

Yeah, that was it. People go shopping in their bathrobes all the time.

7.

By THE NEXT MORNING, I hadn't forgotten about the old woman, exactly, but I'd come to view her presence in the photograph as a bit of random weirdness. Frankly, I had too many real-life worries crowding my head to give her much thought. The most immediate of my concerns: I'd been in town only two days, and I already owed someone money.

Psychic Photo's purple door was open even though a sign taped to it said PLEASE KEEP DOOR CLOSED. Once again, I felt that peculiar sense of well-being when I stepped inside, like the air was filled with the faintest, soothing humming, the frequency just outside my hearing range.

A man in flowered swim trunks stood at the photo printer. "So I just push this button?" he asked Delilah. His voice was high for a man's.

"Yup."

"And then . . . ?"

"You can crop or zoom, same as last time." She was sitting on a stool, engrossed in something on the counter.

"What about if I don't like this shot? Do I still need to print it?" He sounded worried.

"Nope," she mumbled, her eyes still downcast.

"Then what do I do?"

"Hit 'next.'"

I pulled the door closed behind me. The bell jingled.

Delilah looked up. "Hey." She tucked a strand of striped hair behind a twice-pierced ear.

"I brought your money." I'd found sixty bucks in my wallet— just enough to cover the repair.

I crossed to the counter. There was the wooden plank I'd seen the day before, only now it was painted two shades of green. Delilah had glued rows of round objects to the board and decorated them with polka dots and swirls. Loose straws lay scattered around.

"That's . . . interesting," I said. "In a good way."

"It's a lollipop farm. Get it?" She pivoted the plank so I could get a better look, eyes narrowed as if she was testing my reaction.

I stared at the board, and the round objects seemed to take on a new form. "I do."

Weird: when I'd seen the umbrellas on the beach, I thought they looked like a field of lollipops. It had seemed like such a random thought at the time—like something that no one else would come up with. If I believed in all that psychic stuff, I'd wonder if maybe . . . Oh, never mind.

"It took me weeks to collect enough Snapple caps," Delilah said, brushing one with her fingertip. Her nails were painted midnight blue, and she was wearing all of her silver rings again. "I considered making do with some AriZona Iced Tea, but I was going for uniformity in the design."

"Why not just buy a case of Snapple?" I asked.

Delilah wrinkled her nose. "That would be cheating—even if I could afford a case of Snapple, which I can't. My focus right now is on found art."

"Found art?"

She checked my face again, considering me once more, before continuing. "I find a bunch of objects—on the street, on the beach—and then I transform them into art. Bottle caps, old napkins, squished pennies from the railroad track—that kind of thing. Last year I found a headless Barbie doll in the sand. It was like she was waiting for me."

"You mean . . . trash?"

"More like recycling. But I like to think of it as a treasure hunt. Finding the materials is the first part of the creative process."

I felt a spark of recognition. "You know, that's kind of like photography. You never know what you're going to find. You don't make a shot—you discover it."

"*Exactly*," she said.

"What color is your hair naturally?" I blurted, forgetting for the moment that you don't say stuff like that to people you've just met. For some reason, it felt like I'd known Delilah for years but just hadn't placed her. Like, we'd been in preschool together or gymnastics or Girl Scouts or something and we were just waiting for the moment when we'd figure out how we knew each other.

She looked up at her striped bangs. "I've been dying my hair so long, I can't even remember what color it used to be."

38

I stuck a hand in my beach bag, pulled out my plaid wallet, and extracted three twenties. "Anyway, here's the money I owe you."

She abandoned her art and shuffled through a pile of yellow papers until she found my invoice. "That'll be . . . twenty-one dollars and twenty cents."

I shook my head. "It was fifty-three." I didn't want her to discover the error later and think I'd cheated her.

Her mouth twitched. In addition to the freckles that ran across her nose, there was a faint constellation above her mouth. It looked kind of like the Big Dipper.

"That was the estimate. This is the actual cost."

I glanced at the yellow slip. The original amount had been very obviously scratched out.

"I don't want to get you in trouble," I said—though twenty-one dollars was sounding really, really good to me.

She raised her pale, feathery eyebrows. "I don't follow."

"Wouldn't your mother get mad?"

She hooted. "Funny."

I didn't really know what she meant by that, but I handed her the cash, suddenly afraid she was going to say she'd been joking and of course I owed her more.

The guy in the flowered swim trunks was still at the photo machine. "I just zoomed and cropped. Now what do I do?" He rubbed the back of his neck as if he was fending off a stress headache.

"If you want to save the picture, hit *save*." Delilah took my bills and handed back some coins.

The man looked up again. He had a kind face below light, baby-fine hair. "And then what do I do?"

"Hit *next*," Delilah said pleasantly. "Like the last twenty times," she muttered under her breath.

The bells on the door jingled, and a tall, skinny orange boy came in. Seriously. His wavy hair was bright orange and fell just below his chin, while his pinkish face was splattered with freckles. His pants, cut off at mid-calf, were orange, too. He looked like a walking sunset. At least his T-shirt was white. The skateboard under his arm was a disappointing gray.

"Mom here?" he asked Delilah.

"In the back. Getting ready for a reading."

He rolled his eyes. "Lighting candles and burning incense?"

"No more incense," Delilah said. "Not since it gave that woman the asthma attack last week."

"Bad karma," the boy said.

"Totally."

"Can I zoom out?" the guy at the machine asked in his high voice. "Or only zoom in?"

"You can zoom out once you zoom in," the redheaded boy said. "But you can't zoom out from the original shot."

"Why not?"

The boy wiped some sweat off of his pink forehead. "There's nothing you can zoom out to. You've only got what's already in the picture."

The man's eyes widened like he'd just been told the secret of life. "You're right," he said in wonder.

"Madison, this is my brother," Delilah said to me.

"Samson?" It just popped out.

Delilah scowled. "Ha, ha, funny."

"You've heard that one before." I wished I could take it back.

"Almost as many times as the psychic jokes."

"I'm Leonardo," the boy said.

"After the artist?"

He wiggled his orange eyebrows. "The turtle."

That made me smile. "Who's older?"

"I am," Leonardo said. "By a year and a half."

"I'm fifteen," Delilah said.

"Really? Me, too."

She nodded as if she knew that already. "A lot of people think I'm, like, twelve."

"I didn't think that," I said, far too quickly. I looked at Leonardo's orange hair and then at Delilah's striped locks. "Your natural hair color?" I guessed.

She raised her pale eyebrows and tucked a striped lock behind her ear. "Who's to say what's natural?" She turned to Leonardo. "What are you up to?"

He shifted his skateboard to the other arm. "Me and Duncan are going down to the beach to skate. I think I'm late."

"Duncan and I," she said.

Leonardo rolled his eyes. "What. Ever."

"Who's Duncan?" I asked, though it was none of my business.

"Our virtual brother," Delilah said.

I nodded as if that made total sense even if I wondered: *Hologram? Imaginary friend?* Nothing these two said would surprise me much.

The bells on the front door jingled again, and a youngish woman in a loose beach cover-up—yellow patterned with blue fish—clomped over to the man at the printer.

She put her hand on his back. "What's taking you so long? I

was getting worried." A straw beach bag hung from her shoulder.

"This picture stuff is complicated." He peered at the screen.

"It's really not." She smiled patiently and pushed some buttons. Her hair was the same sandy color as her husband's.

I thought of my camera. I hadn't planned on telling anyone about the old woman in the beach shot because it sounded so Sci Fi channel. But it was probably just some technical snafu. Maybe Delilah and Leonardo could explain it to me.

As I fiddled with the case, I tried to keep my voice casual. "After I got my camera back yesterday, I took some shots on the beach. And there was this weird thing. I mean, maybe it's not that weird, but I've never seen it before. . . ."

I turned on the camera and found the picture of the old woman in the pink bathrobe. Delilah and Leonardo peered at it while I told them what had happened.

"You're right," Leonardo said when I'd finished explaining. "It is weird."

"Could something have happened during the repair?" I asked. "Like, maybe someone took a test shot to see if it was working?"

"On the beach?" Delilah said. "No." She wrinkled her freckly nose, scrunching the constellation above her lip. "Have you ever seen this lady, Leo?"

"No." He wrinkled his nose in exactly the same way. "But she looks . . . bright."

"You mean smart?" I asked.

He shook his head. "No, I mean bright—like, light. See? Everything around her is dim and foggy. But she looks like she's standing in a patch of sunshine."

He was right. Normally I pay close attention to the lighting

42

of my photographs, but I'd been so freaked out by the woman's presence that I hadn't even noticed that she seemed to have come out of a different, better-lit shot. Which brought me right back to explanation number three: technical difficulties.

"There must be something funny going on with my memory card," I said. "Like, maybe the last time I downloaded my photos onto my computer, the camera got infected with some kind of virus."

"That makes no sense," Delilah said.

"Maybe she's a ghost," Leonardo suggested, just as the bell on the front door jingled. As I looked up, I half expected to see the woman in the pink bathrobe float into the room.

Instead, it was a guy about my age, shorter than Leonardo, lean and wiry. He looked vaguely familiar. He had tan, almost golden skin and bright green eyes. His hair was brown and wavy-wild, the tips bleached whitish blond. A tiny gold hoop hung in each earlobe. His clothes were standard-issue skater boy: loose, dark T-shirt and long shorts.

He was really cute if you liked that type.

"Dude," he said to Leonardo. "I've been waiting for you for, like, an hour."

"Complications," Leonardo said.

The guy's green eyes shot to me, stopped and grew wide. Blood rushed to my face—and then I realized where I had seen him before.

"The girl on the sidewalk," he said, still looking at me. Of course: he was the guy who'd almost run me down with his skateboard.

"Hi." I looked at the floor, my face still hot for reasons I couldn't understand. He was the one who should have been embarrassed, not me. Because surely that's all I was feeling: embarrassed.

"Madison, this is Duncan," Delilah said. "Our virtual brother." So he wasn't an imaginary friend.

"You met his dad," Delilah told me. "Remember Larry? The guy who fixed your camera?"

I said, "So Larry and your mother are . . ."

"He's her boyfriend," Delilah said. "Or maybe ex-boyfriend. It changes from week to week."

Duncan said, "My dad said it's over. But he was, like, doing her laundry when he said it, so who knows."

"Larry has settling-down issues," Delilah said. "And my mother has commitment issues."

"But she's made a commitment to working on her commitment issues," Leonardo chimed in. "Jury's still out on Larry." Skateboard under his arm, he opened the front door. "Let's boogie," he told Duncan.

Suddenly, the walls shook with thunder.

"So much for the beach," I said.

Duncan's green eyes glittered. "Are you kidding? This is the best time to be there."

I was about to follow Leonardo and Duncan out the door when I noticed the computer on the counter, looking all unused and lonely.

"Would it be okay if I checked my e-mail really fast?" I asked Delilah.

She shrugged. "Sure."

I hope she didn't think it was rude of me to ask—which it was, kind of—but I was feeling seriously out of touch.

44

On MySpace, I had a comment from Rolf Reinhardt, the guy I'd almost, sort of, gone out with in the spring.

heard u made the buzz! awesome! me too—sports reporter.

I'd heard Rolf was on the paper, but I hadn't said anything to him about it. I clicked over to his page (his profile shot showed SpongeBob, which was neither funny nor original) and congratulated myself on not checking to see if he'd posted any new photographs. But, okay, I did glance at his relationship status: single! No way! He and Celia had broken up already!

Not that I cared.

I ran through about twenty possible return comments before finally settling on a simple "congratz."

I had a new message—which I thought was a good thing until I saw Kyle Ziegenfuss's pale, puffy face on the profile shot, his eyes half closed, like he'd just been smoking pot. Which he probably had.

hi madison, just thowt I woud stop by and say hi howz ur summer going mines good, but boring to, wat are u doing this summer, im just hangin call me if u want to hang sometime, kyle

Kyle and I weren't friends, but he didn't quite get that. At Amerige High, I was a "student guide" in this tutoring program called Peerage. Motto: "Bridging the Academic Gap while Building Friendships." Yeah, whatever. Like *The Buzz*, it would help me get into college (again: not that that was my motivation). Basically, the program matched up a smart kid with a dumb kid so the smart kid could make the dumb kid smarter and the dumb kid could make the smart kid more sensitive or something. And I know "dumb kid" sounds really harsh, but it's the term Kyle always used, and, well—you've got to admire his forthrightness. Kyle was classified as learning disabled, which was different than being stupid. But he was seriously slow—in the way he talked, moved, and thought. Maybe he was just unmotivated. More likely, all that pot smoking (he'd started when he was *twelve*) had messed up his brain.

He was a nice enough guy, though, and I didn't want to hurt his feelings, so I always answered his messages.

hi kyle,
thx 4 stopping by! i'm away 4 most of the summer.
hope u r having a gr8 time.
madison

At least spending the summer in Sandyland meant I didn't have to worry about running into Kyle. I hit *send* and sighed.

"Bad news?" Delilah asked, gluing a straw to her board.

"Nah, just—there's this guy, and . . ." I tried to come up with the right words.

"Boyfriend?"

"Kyle?" I shuddered. "God, no. He just thinks we're closer than we really are, and I don't want to hurt his feelings, but . . ." I shook my head. "Whatever. I don't have to deal with him till September."

"September?"

"When I go back to school."

She said, "But in September you'll be—" And then she stopped.

"What?" I asked.

"Nothing." She looked at the counter, and I started to feel all creeped out, like maybe Delilah could see my future. But that was ridiculous. She wasn't even the family psychic—not that I believed in any of that stuff.

As I left the shop, I heard the printer whir to life.

"See? That was easy," the sandy-haired woman told her husband. And then, to Delilah: "How much would it cost to have my fortune told?"

8.

OVER THE NEXT FEW DAYS:

It rained.

I learned more than I ever wanted to know about sharks.

And my mother got a job.

Let's start with the rain. After a long night of pounding water, wall-shaking thunder, and flashbulb-bright lightning, a stagnant, damp dreariness turned the sky a murky, one-tone gray and unleashed the full power of Home Suite Home's mildewed dog aroma. It was the kind of rain that ruled out long walks or picture taking. It was the kind of rain that dulled hope and cut vacations short.

Not that we were on vacation.

In the motel parking lot, dads in Windbreakers ran back and forth loading minivans and SUVs while shivering children stood damp-faced in open doorways, cartoons blasting from behind.

Homesickness struck me like a terrible flu. My muscles ached and my stomach cramped. I wanted my bed, my computer, my photo-covered walls. I wanted my kitchen and den and living room.

I wanted my life.

We couldn't see a movie or go shopping or do any of the other stuff I typically did on a rainy day—because, in case I hadn't heard my parents the first fifty times, "money is tight" and "we all need to make sacrifices." (Argh!) Not that it mattered: the closest movie theater was miles away, and the surf shop was the only store worth visiting. There wasn't even a bookstore in town, and I'd already finished the two books I'd brought.

So I filled the time listening to my iPod, taking still-life photos of bruised fruit in a purple plastic bowl, and watching "Shark Week" on the Discovery Channel. Part of the programming was dedicated to explaining how rare shark attacks are. A larger part was spent on shark attack reenactments, with the occasional *Jaws* clip thrown in. It was enough to turn me from an Ocean Person to a Lake Person.

My father, slumped on the edge of his bed in a T-shirt and shorts (at least he'd changed out of his bathrobe), watched every minute. He was supposed to be working—that's why we were here, after all—but it was raining too hard for construction.

In case sharks weren't scary enough, late in the day the programming gave way to haunted house investigations. Ghosts scratched children's cheeks. They hovered over beds. They rattled pipes, shattered dishes, blew cold air.

"Get out of the house!" I muttered at the television. If these people were so terrified, why didn't they just pack up their bags and go?

Why couldn't we?

During the commercials, I played with my camera. Most of my Sandyland shots were the usual beach stuff: breaking waves, the yellow swim float, some long-legged sandpipers. Again and again,

I returned to the old woman in the pink bathrobe. She was still there. It still made no sense.

Maybe she's a ghost.

Leonardo was just saying that. Ghosts aren't real. Everyone knows that, even the people on TV. If ghosts were real, those people would get out of their houses.

Grocery shopping with my mother was the highlight of my first rainy day; that's how low I had sunk. Outside Food World there were gumball machines, a coin-powered pony, and a blue charity drop-off bin with CLOTHING AND SHOES ONLY stenciled on the side. After wearing my black shorts and pink-and-black-striped T-shirt for four days straight, I longed to pitch them into the bin. Unfortunately, that would leave me naked.

Inside the store, it was freezing. Overhead, fluorescent lights buzzed as if they, too, were shivering. My mom pushed the squeaky cart while I used my honors math skills—imperfect though they were—to comparison shop. We hardly spoke. When she muttered, "I suppose I should start clipping coupons," it took all my strength not to say, "Yeah, that'll fix everything."

In the health and beauty aisle, she spent some time looking at hair color boxes before picking one called ASH BLONDE. And then she shocked me by asking, "Do you want to do yours, too?"

This was a peace offering. I'd been asking for blond streaks since junior high. I reached for a highlighting kit and then stopped. Blond streaks seemed too cheery for my current mood.

Instead, I took a box of black dye off the shelf, narrowing my eyes at my mother, daring her to stop me. But she didn't say anything.

On our way to the check stand, we passed the "Flower Shoppe," which was basically a counter with plastic buckets full of carnations and daisies, along with shiny balloons that said HAPPY BIRTHDAY and CONGRATULATIONS ON YOUR RETIREMENT.

My mother paid for the groceries in cash. For a moment, I worried that she wouldn't have enough money—how mortifying would that be?—but she did. When the checkout woman gave her the change, my mother cleared her throat and asked, "Are you hiring?"

That floored me. When my mother had said she was getting a job, I thought she meant something glamorous, like an interior designer or a party planner. And I guess I thought she meant something easy to leave. A real job, with regular hours, tied us to this town more than I liked. She was going to make me stay here for the entire summer. I could just feel it.

"Applications are at customer service," the checkout woman told her.

My mother nodded but did not stop on the way out. "I want to color my hair first," she told me.

"No rush," I said.

"Ash Blonde" was misnamed. It should have been called "Margarine."

"Maybe you can find a salon around here to fix it," I said when my mother came out of the bathroom, a stained white towel over her shoulders.

I was just trying to be helpful, but the wrinkle between her eyebrows deepened. "You want me to do yours?" she asked.

I touched a strand of my brown hair. On the way home from Food World, I'd decided that black hair was a bad idea. But I didn't want to back out and hand my mother even the tiniest victory.

She ripped open the cardboard box and put on plastic gloves. There were two bottles; she poured the smaller one into the larger and shook it. Immediately, the room stank: a harsh chemical smell that made my nose sting.

I closed my eyes and pictured Jenny, my hairdresser back home. She was twenty-five, with streaky hair cut in daring angles. Now, far from the salon, my mother drew stripes along my scalp with a plastic bottle. When she'd worked her way from ear to ear, she stroked the goo along the length of my brown hair and then snapped a plastic shower cap over the whole smelly mess.

While I waited, I washed my black shorts and striped T-shirt in the bathroom sink with the bug-spray-scented shampoo. When I was done, I wrung them out as best as I could and hung them on the towel bar to dry. I could wear my Dennis's Building Supply T-shirt until morning.

Later, as I stood in the shower, the water ran gray at my feet. I got scalded just once as someone, somewhere, flushed a toilet. But that wasn't the worst of it. My hair looked bad wet. Dry, it looked hideous, like a Halloween wig—and not a nice one from a party store, either, but a cheap one that you'd pick up at the drugstore for six bucks.

"I told you black was a bad idea," my mother said when she saw it.

"No, you didn't."

"You know what I thought."

My clothes were still damp the next (rainy) morning. I tried on all of the outgrown clothes my parents had brought on the off chance that I had shrunk.

I hadn't. Most of the clothes were from junior high (I should really clean out my closet more often). The shirts ended above my belly button, and the shorts wouldn't snap.

If only my mother wasn't so stinking skinny, I could have worn some of her clothes. Instead, I was left with my dad's fugly orange T-shirt (which he'd told me I could keep—gee, thanks—because it was too small for him anyway) and my new board shorts. *It's not like I'm going to run into anyone I know.* An image of that skater boy, Duncan, flashed through my mind.

Not my type.

When my mother went back to Food World to submit her application, I tagged along with the shopping bag full of my old clothes. The bag fell with a hollow thump inside the blue charity bin: a piece of my life gone forever.

"You can wait out here, if you want," my mother said, standing by the automatic door as I adjusted my board shorts, which really were kind of big. Beyond us, raindrops trickled from the eaves.

I shrugged. "I'll go in." It's not like I had anything better to do.

Her nostrils flared, and that's when I saw myself as she did: the wiggy black hair, the baggy T-shirt. I was fifteen years old and my mother was ashamed to be seen with me. Talk about ironic.

The store called the next day (still raining: day three of my captivity) to offer my mother a job as Floral Shoppe Assistant. They'd been impressed with her experience arranging centerpieces for charity league luncheons and PTA fund-raisers. Also, they were surprised that she knew what a hydrangea was.

"Did you tell them it was just for the summer?" I asked.

She didn't answer. But then, she was busy making dinner, so maybe she just didn't hear me.

9.

ON FRIDAY I WOKE TO SUNNY SKIES. Well, I woke to clear skies. The sun was hardly even up. In the past week, I'd been going to bed earlier and earlier because there was nothing to do at night. The problem was now I couldn't sleep past six or seven.

Early morning at Home Suite Home meant rattling pipes, screaming children, blaring televisions, and yapping dogs. You'd think I'd get used to the sounds, but they kept changing. There were new trucks in need of mufflers, new children with higher pitched screams, new dogs howling at the moon. Small dogs were noisier than big ones and young children whinier than old.

There was another new sound today: my parents getting ready for work, my mother showering, my father drinking his coffee in front of the television. My dad was going to be doing "hands-on labor" on an expensive new house. He did his best to sound enthusiastic.

"A block from the beach, two stories high—you'll be able to see the ocean from the master bedroom. Three thousand square feet, and I know that doesn't sound that big, but it almost fills the entire lot. But before construction, we gotta bury phone and power lines; we gotta dig trenches by hand to protect the existing trees."

From the way he talked, you'd think he was building the house for us.

I hung around for about an hour after my parents left. It was nice to be alone, but after being stuck inside for so many days, I was dying to get out of that place. In the bathroom I pulled my black shorts and black-and-pink tee off the towel rack. They were still damp and kind of stretched out. Even worse, they smelled like mildew. But it was that or the orange T-shirt/board shorts combo, and I'd come to hate Dennis of Dennis's Building Supply almost as much as I hated Sandyland—though not as much as I hated my parents for ruining my summer in the first place.

When I glanced at the mirror, I jumped at the stranger looking back. I'd completely forgotten about my black hair. A good night's sleep—well, a bad night's sleep (have I mentioned how much I despised the couch?)—had done nothing to improve my new look.

On the plus side, with hair so breathtakingly hideous, maybe no one would notice that my clothes smelled.

As I walked to the main street, the sun popped above the horizon and spread a golden light over everything. Just as I thought, *It's pretty here*, a foul-tempered cloud took over and turned the world back to gray. So much for taking pictures.

Downtown Sandyland was quiet. Most shops—and all

"shoppes"—were closed. An open door led to an Internet café. Entering, I took in the intoxicating aroma of coffee and the raindrop rhythm of tapping keys. For an Internet café, it was a little short on computers, but there were plenty of tables and chairs, all mismatched and painted bright colors. A glass bakery case displayed muffins, scones, and pastries.

I bought a vanilla latte and a half hour of Internet time. It put a pretty good-sized dent into my life savings, but you only live once—if you're lucky, that is. The past week felt like a second life, and so far it wasn't working out so well.

First, I went to Google and typed in "ghosts in photos." After that, I tried "spirits in photos" and "unexplained figures in photos."

There were tons of hits. I pored over the photos of shadowy figures looming in the distance, translucent bodies hovering at the edge. None of the ghostly figures were half as clear as the lady in the pink bathrobe. They looked more like fog or smoke. Most of the photos were really old, taken with black-and-white film. Any idiot could see that the "ghosts" weren't real—just some obvious double exposures or tricks of the light.

I tried a new search: "ghosts in digital pictures." I found a few ghost hunter sites debating the merits of digital photography— but, again, the pictures showed misty white figures that looked nothing like my shots.

This was ridiculous. The lady in my photo didn't look like the pictures online for a simple reason: ghosts aren't real.

As I logged on to my MySpace account, I felt almost normal. There was my profile name (Mad Girl) and my profile picture, which showed Lexie and me with our identical haircuts, hers blond, mine its old natural brown. We were laughing at something absolutely hysterical. (What was it? It bothered me that I couldn't remember.)

There was my profile song, my list of favorite television shows, books, and movies. In the Top Friends box, familiar faces smiled back at me.

Naturally I'd posted a lot of photos on my page. I stared at them like a stalker. Some were of my friends goofing around. A couple showed me smiling, with no idea what lay ahead. There were scenes of Amerige: arty photos of flower gardens and windows, stop signs and benches.

There were no ghosts anywhere.

On the bottom right, a bunch of people from school had left me comments. My first reaction was relief: nothing from Kyle Ziegenfuss!

And then I started reading.

hey mad, howz yr summer? did u go on yr cruise yet? i am sooo jealous. text me if u get this.

whassup madison? where u been hiding? yr cell sayz its disconnected. u got a new #?

I'd have to post a bulletin or something to tell everyone that I was spending the whole summer at the beach. They didn't have to know why. At least I'd have a good tan when I went back to school in September.

hi madison, so weird! i walked by yr house

**yesterday & there were all thez ppl out front. were
you having a yd sale or sumthing? ur not moving
r u???? maybe I got the wrong house but I think it
was yrs.**

Huh? That was strange. Maybe my parents were having work done on our house while we were gone. But that didn't make any sense. Why would they spend the money there if we were *here* because they don't have any? Besides, my dad had been sitting around for months. If something needed painting or fixing, he would have done it himself.

**yo mad! whas goin' on? weirdest thing—ppl keep
saying yr moving, that yr house is for sale & u don't
even live there anymore.**

My palms began to sweat. What was going on? My parents wouldn't sell the house without telling me. Would they?

No—there's no way my mother would leave that house. She'd made my father paint the living room four times just to get the perfect shade of yellow. She'd hired a cabinetmaker to build custom shelving in The Library and a seamstress to sew curtains for all of the windows.

There must be some mistake.

In addition to the comments, there were new messages. I was almost afraid to read them, but I had eight minutes of Internet time left, and I couldn't let them go to waste.

Two messages were from Melissa Raffman, editor of *The Buzz*. The first was from a couple days ago.

58

Madison,

I'm really excited that you'll be joining us on the newspaper staff. Your photos will be an excellent contribution.

As I mentioned, I'm planning to host a staff get-together at my house in the next couple of weeks. I'll call you when the details are finalized. Can you give me your cell number? The number I had on file didn't work.

Thanks,

Melissa

Melissa's second message had just been posted.

Madison,

Someone mentioned that your house was being sold. Can I assume you are moving to another house in town? I've tried to reach you on your home phone, but it has been disconnected.

If you are not going to be attending Amerige High in the fall, please let me know as soon as possible so I can offer the photography position to someone else.

Melissa

My home phone was disconnected? Panic spread through my chest for just a moment before I figured it out. My parents hadn't paid the bill. The phone company had cut off our service. This was seriously embarrassing. Suddenly, my virtual world sucked almost as much as my real world. At least the virtual me still had good hair.

> Hi Melissa,
> I'm out of town for the summer (my parents rented a place at the beach), but I'll be back before school starts. Hate to miss the party. Tell everyone I said hi!
> Can't wait to start work on the paper. Thanks for picking me.
> Madison
> P.S. Don't know what's going on with the phone, but there's been some construction on our street, and sometimes that messes things up.

My last new message was from Lexie. I read it fast because time was ticking away and I didn't want to surrender any future latte funds.

> mad cow,
> 1. the lake sux. brooke got bit by a fly & it got infected & my dad had to take her to the e.r. & now I'm stuck w/kenzie in my room cuz brooke is supposedly moaning & crying in her sleep. such a faker. u r so lucky 2 b an only child.
> 2. i got the inside scoop about celia & rolf. 2 many details 4 here, but she dumped him & then changed her mind but he wouldn't take her back. now she is crying 2 everyone about how

she LUVS him. she is so gross.
3. got a weird message from melissa on my cell.
she wanted 2 know if u had moved. i called & said
no (duh). u shd probably call her.
luv from your bff & the prisoner of the lake,
lex-mex

I dashed off a quick note to Lexie, trying to ignore the fear that pricked the back of my neck.

lex-mex,
1. no sympathy. none. the parental units have
decided to extend our va-cay @ the lamest beach
on earth.
2. celia will die alone. does rolf like anyone now?
3. weird. melissa must have called the wrong #. i
just sent her a message so all is good.
luv from yr bff & prisoner of the beach,
mad cow

As if on cue, when my Internet time ran out, the sun popped above the clouds, and I rushed to the beach. The sun was like a magic spotlight, its beams gold with just the slightest hint of pink. Everything it touched turned beautiful. Even the trash cans were striking, as long as you thought of them as simple shapes: three green cylinders standing in a row, perfectly spaced, a wooden fence running in parallel lines behind them.

Snap.

"You cutting in on my territory?" Delilah stood to one side, a plastic grocery bag in each hand, smiling. She was wearing a yellow cotton dress with short, puffy sleeves and a row of buttons down the front.

"Hey," I said. My face flushed at the thought of my black hair—which, even now, wasn't as weird as Delilah's, but still. Seeing her plastic bags, I remembered what she'd said about scavenging materials for her art. "You find anything good?"

She peered inside. "Styrofoam, mostly: coffee cups and some of those take-out containers. I'll wash them with bleach when I get home so they don't smell. I'm speaking from experience."

"Are you going to add them to the piece you were working on the other day?"

She shook her striped head. "Nah, the lollipop field is almost done. This is raw material for my next piece, which I plan to call *Landfill*. Last week, I found a busted boogie board on the beach; that'll be my canvas. I'll use the Styrofoam to build a series of hills, which I'll cover with different things: aluminum foil, hamburger wrappers, whatever I can find." She paused. "I haven't figured it out beyond that. But it'll make some kind of an environmental statement."

She pointed at my head. "I like your hair."

That was a bit like having a blind person compliment my photography, but whatever. "Thanks."

"Your camera working okay?" she asked.

"Yeah. I still can't figure out how that old woman turned up in a shot, though. Anyway, I haven't been able to take many pictures because of the rain."

She motioned down the beach. "You might want to come back tomorrow. Saturdays, the town rents kayaks—over there, by that

62

little gray house. They're all different colors, and I always thought they looked cool lined up on the sand. I mean, not as cool as the trash cans, but—you know."

I checked her face to see if she was making fun of me, but she meant it about the trash cans. The girl liked her trash. I looked down the beach and tried to imagine the kayaks. It would be fun to play around with the shapes, the colors.

"Thanks for the tip," I said. "I'll check it out."

"And also tomorrow . . ." She looked down shyly. "There's this excellent thrift store downtown. I get most of my clothes there." That explained a lot.

"It's only open on Saturdays," she said. "I was planning on going tomorrow—it opens at nine—so if you want to meet me there. . . ."

Used clothes? Yuck. I went to the Salvation Army a couple of years ago when I needed a costume for the school play, and everything just smelled . . . weird. Like dust mixed with perfume mixed with death. I didn't want to offend Delilah, but that whole "vintage" thing was way overrated.

"Saturday . . . hmm," I said, as if trying to recall the details of my busy schedule. The breeze blew my hair in front of my face. It felt like a cobweb. I reached up to tuck the hair behind my ear and that's when I caught the smell, almost beachlike but not quite. It was the mildew from my still-damp clothes. Humiliation washed over me.

"My parents forgot to put my suitcase in the car," I said. "That's why I'm always wearing the same thing. But I've got lots of other stuff at home."

"Of course!" she said. "I didn't mean . . . what I meant was . . .

you know. There's not a lot going on around here, so it's just something to do."

The breeze blew again, releasing an even stronger mildew aroma. I wanted to rip my clothes off and throw them in the ocean. Next week my dad would go to Amerige and bring back my suitcase. Next week sounded far away.

"The thrift shop sounds . . . fun," I said.

We walked down the beach, gazing at the ground, finding treasures everywhere. A yellow shovel. A button. An empty suntan lotion bottle. Delilah ignored a damp magazine but snatched up the *National Enquirer*. "The headlines are like gold," she said. "Look at this: 'Worst Beach Bodies.' I could glue the headline on a board and then stick some Barbie dolls next to it. Wish I'd saved the headless one. . . ."

I snapped pictures of the yellow shovel, of a volleyball net, a lone beach chair. After each shot I paused to check my display, but there was nothing out of place, no old woman hovering at the edge.

The sun rose higher in the sky; the light became harsh. I put my camera away. The kids in the red bathing suits began to appear, alone and in groups. A tall blond guy, Hollywood gorgeous with a perfect jock body, walked by and smiled. "Hey, Delilah." He carried a surfboard under his arm and wore a whistle around his neck. He looked like he was on his way to a Hollister photo shoot.

"Hi, Nate," she said casually. When he was out of earshot, she whispered, "You can't beat the scenery on the beach."

When we got back to the sandy parking lot, all the spots were filled with minivans and SUVs. The sun was high in the sky, the air getting hotter by the minute. Delilah's pale skin flushed pink.

"Yo, Dee!" Leonardo and Duncan sat on a green bench, skateboards at their feet, both of them eating. Leonardo's pants were red today. His T-shirt was bright blue. His hair was still the natural, crazy orange. Still, it looked better than my hair. I wished I'd worn a hat. I wished I owned a hat.

"Hey, guys." Delilah strode over. "Leo, you got some food for me?"

Across the parking lot, a line snaked away from the snack shack's take-out window. The smell of fried food tortured my hungry nose.

Cheeseburger clutched securely in his other hand, Leonardo held out a Styrofoam container filled with fries. "Don't take too many."

Delilah took a monster fistful and skittered away.

"Hey!" Leonardo said.

She laughed. "I have to share with Madison." She looked at me. "Want some?"

I wasn't sure what to do. It seemed kind of rude to eat Leo's food; I barely even knew him. But I'd had nothing but the vanilla latte all day, and I was starving. Besides, I liked having Delilah treat me like a friend. I couldn't imagine hanging out with her in real life, but she was perfect for an arty summer companion.

I accepted a fry from her outstretched hand, trying not to think of how recently that hand had been in a garbage can.

"You can have some of mine," Duncan said, holding out his overflowing Styrofoam shell. He wore long khaki shorts and a white T-shirt with the sleeves cut off, revealing lean, muscled arms.

"No, thanks." I knew Duncan even less well than I knew Leo.

"Have a fry." He leaned forward. His gold earrings glinted in the sunlight. "C'mon, Goth Girl; you know you want one."

"*Goth Girl?*" I stared at him, mouth open. Okay, sure—with the hair, shirt, and shorts I was a little over the top on the black, but I had *not* crossed the line into Gothic. And Duncan, with his wild hair bleached white at the tips, was hardly one to talk.

A family walked by, hauling enough beach toys for fifty children.

"Or how about I just call you G.G.?" Duncan said. "The black hair is totally working for you, by the way."

At my stunned expression he cracked up. His laugh was infectious—like a series of hiccups, almost.

I started laughing and couldn't stop. It was the first time I'd laughed in almost a week, and I poured everything into it: my fear, my anxiety, and a moment's relief and release. Delilah and Leonardo joined in, probably amused by my overreaction more than anything, and I laughed even harder, tears forming in my eyes.

Finally, I composed myself and plopped down on the bench next to Duncan, entirely forgetting about my smelly clothes. "Scoot over." He slid closer to Leo. I peered at his food. "Screw the fries," I said, tucking my black hair behind my ears. "I want some of your burger."

I took the burger in both hands and took a shamelessly huge bite. It was just the way I liked it, with lettuce and cheese, grilled onions, and Russian dressing. It was quite possibly the best burger I had ever tasted, though that may have just been because I was so hungry. Or maybe it was the setting: when the sun was shining, Sandyland didn't suck at all.

Still chewing, I tried to give Duncan back his burger, but he just said, "Nah, have more." My second bite was slightly less greedy than my first, my third bordering on normal.

"I lived in a town called Madison once," Duncan said after I finally insisted he take the burger back (trying really hard not to gaze longingly at the remaining half). "Is that your real name?"

It was kind of a weird question. "Well, yeah," I said, licking my lips. "Isn't Duncan your real name?"

"Nope." He took a small bite of his burger and then held it out to me. "Finish it."

I checked his expression to make sure he was serious about the burger, and then I reached for it slowly, as if he might snatch it away. "You really don't want it?" Of course he wanted the burger. Why else would he have ordered it?

"I'll eat the fries."

My hunger was so intense that I gobbled the burger quickly, before I had a chance to feel guilty.

"So, what's your real name, then?" I asked, using the back of my hand to wipe grease off my mouth in an extremely ladylike fashion.

"I'd tell you." He held my gaze with his green, green eyes. "But then I'd have to kill you."

A smile tugged at my mouth. "That would be a waste of a perfectly good burger."

He grinned, and his green eyes crinkled.

"Is Duncan your middle name, then?" I asked, suddenly curious.

"Nope. I named myself."

"After the character in *Macbeth*?"

He raised his eyebrows. "The donuts."

Donuts. Mmm.

He said, "Used to be, I'd pick a new name every time I moved. But that got confusing. I've stuck with Duncan for a while now." He plucked a ketchup-drenched fry from the Styrofoam container and popped it in his mouth.

"How many times have you moved?"

He looked up, thinking. "Twenty-four times? Maybe twenty-three."

Twenty-three moves? I shuddered. "Wow. I've only moved once, and it was in the same town."

A gray gull swooped past before circling back to land near our feet. Duncan tossed a fry, and the bird pounced.

He said, "I'm on my eleventh school, I know that. There'd be more, but my father *homeschooled* me for a couple of years." When he said "homeschooled," he held his fingers up in quotation marks.

"But he's not moving anymore," Delilah said. "We're keeping him. My mom said he can stay with us, even if his dad takes off."

Duncan didn't respond, just chucked a few final fries onto the asphalt before closing up his empty Styrofoam shell. Squawking gulls swooped in from every angle to battle over the scraps.

"You could've given those fries to me," Delilah said.

"What about your mom?" I asked Duncan.

"She joined a cult," he said, as if he were talking about a job transfer. He stood up from the bench and headed for the nearest trash can.

"Don't throw that out," Delilah said, reaching for the container. Duncan gave it to her without question and took his place next to me on the bench. Maybe it was just my imagination, but it seemed like he was sitting closer to me than before.

"A cult," I said, hungry for details but trying hard to keep all traces of "that's whacked" out of my voice.

"When I was three," he said. "It wasn't really her fault. She just fell in with this weird-ass crowd, and they just, like, brainwashed her."

Leonardo, his food all gone, offered his container to Delilah. "Nah, I got enough," she said. When he walked over to the trash can, she took his seat on the bench. In retaliation, he sat on top of her.

"Get your bony butt off of me!" she yelled, until Duncan pressed himself against my side to make room for her.

"Hey, Madison," Leo called from the far end of the bench. "You find any more ghosts in your pictures?"

Duncan said, "Any more *what?*"

As I powered up my camera, Delilah told Duncan about the mysterious old woman in my photo.

"It's pretty weird," I said, scrolling through the shots on my display screen until I found the old lady by the rocks. "I'm sure she wasn't on the beach."

"Maybe she snuck into the camera when you weren't looking," Duncan said.

I checked his expression. He was kidding, of course. Wasn't he?

"I can ask my dad about it if you want," Duncan said. "I mean, we can get together some time and ask him together."

Leonardo didn't even try to hide his snicker.

I'd planned to talk to my parents about our home phone being out of order, but when my dad walked into the room at the end of the day, his face so red and sweaty and his breathing so labored, I was actually afraid he might be having a heart attack.

"Are you okay?" I asked when he stumbled in and collapsed on the bed. I'd never seen anyone so filthy in my life.

He didn't answer my question, just looked at me with dull eyes. "Water?"

I got him a big glass filled high with ice. He winced when I handed it to him, and he held up his blister-covered palm. He took a long, desperate drink before wiping his mouth and saying, "I'll work hard, and we'll get back on our feet."

He drained the rest of his water and put the glass on the night-stand.

10.

SATURDAY MORNING, I SPENT AT LEAST AN HOUR photographing kayaks (Delilah was right: they did look cool), and then I got to the thrift shop ten minutes early. Delilah was already there, waiting in the parking lot, along with what appeared to be half of Sandyland. It looked like the mob at the mall on the day after Thanksgiving—only without the food court, the ear-piercing kiosk, and the nice clothes that had never been worn.

"Get your elbows ready," Delilah told me, standing at the edge of the crowd.

"Huh?"

"It gets vicious in there." She narrowed her eyes at the other shoppers. There were all ages: moms with little kids, grandparents, teenagers (girls mostly, but not entirely). One of the teenagers was a girl with striped hair similar to Delilah's, though the other girl's stripes were only white. She looked kind of like a zebra.

Today Delilah wore cutoff denim overalls over a tank top. Now that I knew about the thrift shop, I couldn't look at anything she wore without wondering who had owned it first.

I really didn't want to be here.

But I had no choice. I couldn't wait to change out of my mildewed black clothes.

At least this thrift shop, a block off Main Street and next to a pretty white church, was a lot nicer than the blocky, dingy Salvation Army fortress at home. Enormous, leafy trees shaded the little white building with green shutters. *Don't think "used clothes,"* I commanded myself. *Think "vintage." Don't think "poor people." Think "treasure hunters."*

"You need to figure out your strategy," Delilah told me, weaving her fingers together and stretching out her arms. She had her silver rings on, along with a bracelet made out of paper clips. She'd repainted her fingernails, alternating red and black. "Decide what section you want to hit first," she advised.

"I was thinking clothes," I said, the taste of my mom's bitter coffee lingering in my mouth.

"Yeah, but *which* clothes?" Her light eyes widened. "The shirt aisle gets the most traffic, so you might want to hit that first, before all the good stuff is gone. Then, if there's anything worthwhile left, you can move on to jeans, shorts, shoes—whatever."

"But I need everything!" I blurted, forgetting for a moment that I was too good for used clothes.

"Grab some shirts and then head over to the shorts," she counseled. "You'll be fine."

"Morning, Delilah!" A tall, heavy woman stood over us, blocking the morning sun. Bobby pins held back brown hair threaded with gray. Her dress was green with enormous pink flowers. She looked like a walking couch.

"Hello, Mrs. Voorhees."

"Your mom here?" Mrs. Voorhees peered around. "I was hoping to make an appointment." Her voice was high and childish; it didn't match her body at all.

"She didn't come this morning. But she should be in the shop this afternoon if you want to stop by."

"Rose has been guiding me toward a transformational experience," Mrs. Voorhees told us. "And I've been meditating on my own every day, but I feel like I've hit a plateau. I need Rose to help me unleash my inner energy."

"She's good at that," Delilah said, her face neutral.

To keep from cracking up, I looked away and concentrated on my breathing.

Mrs. Voorhees's voice turned sad. "Also, I wanted to tell your mother that Francine Lunardi died yesterday morning." She leaned toward me, forcing eye contact. "Francine's the one who introduced me to Rose."

I nodded.

Mrs. Voorhees gazed into the distance. "Francine never would have held on so long, but last week she finally set things right with her daughter. That gave her the inner peace she needed to let go."

I nodded as if this made sense, my face hurting from politeness.

When the thrift shop's front door swung open, Delilah grabbed my arm and pulled me after her. The store was bigger than it had appeared from the outside, but not by much. Shirts, dresses, and pants were crammed on racks, dishes and glassware jammed on shelves. Dust danced in the rays of sun that sliced through the windows.

Delilah hadn't been kidding about the elbows. Two-dollar shirts turned Sandyland women into animals. The girl with the zebra hair reached for a black T-shirt at the same time I did, but, revved up by the competition, I held tight. We locked eyes. She said, "What. Ever," and released the shirt. She moved on to the next rack, the smell of cigarettes lingering behind her.

Trying on the clothes was out of the question; I just had to hope for the best. I thought I was doing pretty well, having snagged the black shirt, but Delilah scored so much stuff she had to stash it behind the counter so no one would take it.

"Leave some for the rest of us," the girl with the zebra hair grumbled from behind a rack of jeans.

"Lighten up, Jessamine," Delilah said.

By the time we finished, I had three T-shirts (one black, one white, one dark purple with a swirly black design) and two pairs of jeans, one black and one blue.

And Delilah? She'd spent almost fifty dollars without knowing what, exactly, she had bought. "Summer's the best time for the thrift shop," she told me as we trudged toward Main Street. "When the summer people get here, they go through their clothes and decide that everything needs to be replaced."

Psychic Photo was closed, a sign in the window promising an eleven o'clock opening. Delilah led me to a back alley, pulled a key from the pocket of her overalls and jiggled the knob of yet another purple door until it gave with a creak. The door opened onto a little hallway. There was a closed door straight ahead and a set of steep stairs to the right.

"I'm home," Delilah called up the stairs, shrugging when no one answered. She put another key into the door in front of us.

"You live here?" I asked.

"Upstairs," she said. With a grin she added, "Though the energy up there isn't nearly as powerful as it is downstairs."

Rose's Reading Room (Delilah's phrase, not mine) was kind of disappointing: no crystal ball or lamps draped with filmy scarves, just a couple of worn green love seats facing each other, a scratched coffee table in between. Along one wall, next to a beat-up brown mini fridge and a small sink, a folding table held a coffeemaker and a messy pile of paper plates and napkins. An old computer sat on a desk along another wall; a bulky photo-developing machine was crammed into the corner. Everywhere I looked there were cardboard boxes, many of them empty. A headless dressmaker's dummy was the only thing out of place, but I figured it had something to do with Delilah's art.

Delilah emptied her black trash bags onto the gray industrial carpet.

"I have a pair of shorts just like that," I said, spotting a familiar plaid. I felt closer to Delilah all of a sudden, just thinking we owned the same thing. But then I remembered: my plaid Billabong shorts were from eighth grade. I'd dropped them in the charity bin.

I corrected myself: "Well, I used to have shorts like that, anyway. But I gave them away."

As Delilah sorted through the clothes, a T-shirt caught my eye: red with a moose. "Hey—I had a T-shirt like that, too. It was

75

my favorite." And then (a little late, I admit) it hit me. "Those are my clothes!"

"Huh?" Delilah looked up from the floor.

I picked up the Abercrombie shirt and checked the tag. "I dropped a whole bunch of stuff in a charity bin a few days ago. It must have gone to the thrift store. This was my shirt—that's so funny that you bought it! And these shorts were mine, too: Billabong, see? Anything else?" I pawed through the piles until I came up with a white Hollister camisole that had never fit me quite right.

"These were your clothes, and you just threw them away?" Delilah asked, astonished.

"They didn't fit," I said. I squinted at Delilah, who was at least four inches taller than me. And then I gave her the bad news. "They're going to be way too small for you."

She laughed at my misunderstanding. "I'm not going to *wear* them!"

Before I had a chance to ask what, besides wearing, the clothes were good for, the back door swung open. Leonardo and Duncan burst into the room, their arms loaded with . . . What is the word I'm looking for? Oh, yeah: junk.

"We struck gold at the yard sales today," Leonardo announced to the sound of clinking ceramic. "NFL mugs! From the eighties!"

"Hey, G.G.!" Duncan said when he saw me.

"The eighties? Get out!" Delilah chirped, rushing over to see the mugs. "How many?"

"I am not Goth," I informed Duncan. "I'm just having a bad hair month."

"Nothing wrong with Goth," he said. "Oh, Delilah—your

mom said to tell you she's at my place."

"Where's your dad?"

"Out on the boat. He left at, like, four this morning. Your mom made me and Leo pancakes."

"She never makes me pancakes," Delilah grumbled.

"That's because you're so capable," Leonardo said.

"They weren't very good," Duncan assured Delilah. "Kind of rubbery."

Leo put the mugs on the folding table next to the coffeemaker. "I think there's . . ." He counted. "Eleven. But wait." He picked up a plastic grocery bag. "They had some shot glasses, too. New York Giants, Miami Dolphins . . . and . . . Raiders."

"Sweet!" Delilah said.

Leo looked at Duncan. "Where are the Raiders from—San Francisco?"

"Oakland," Duncan said. And to me: "Leo grew up without a father. That's why he's sports-challenged." Duncan smiled at me. I smiled back. He kept smiling. I thought, *Not my type*, and made myself look away.

"And why he wears pink pants," Delilah said.

"They're orange," Leo said, patting his leg. His T-shirt was tie-dyed rainbow hues.

I crept slowly toward the hideous mugs, trying to keep my face neutral.

"I got Pokémon cards," Duncan said, reaching into a pocket of his cargo pants.

Definitely not my type. You'd think that someone old enough to have earrings would be too old for Pokémon.

"Are they rare?" Delilah asked.

77

Duncan shrugged and said what sounded like, "I-uh-no."

"There's no point unless they're rare," Delilah said.

Oh, great. Here I thought I'd found a cool, arty summer friend, and she was a Pokémon expert. Suddenly I missed Lexie so much my stomach hurt. To make things worse, this room smelled funny. Oh, wait: that was me.

"Is there a bathroom I can use?" I asked. "So I can change my clothes?" I still hated the idea of used clothes, but I had to get out of this smelly stuff. And besides, it was just for a few days, until my dad got my suitcase from home.

"It's upstairs," Delilah said, just as Duncan said, "I'll show you!"

He moves like a cat, I thought, following him. Not quite an adult cat—more like an almost-grown kitten: bouncy and graceful at the same time. At the top of the stairs, he reached into a front pocket, and his shoulder blades made sharp angles in his black T-shirt. I had a sudden urge to take his picture, but I didn't want to give him the wrong idea.

He twisted his head to smile at me. One of his front teeth had a little chip. I knocked out part of a tooth when I was eight, and my dentist had it repaired before the next day. But I liked his chipped tooth. It went with his wild brown hair with the white tips. It went with the tiny gold hoops in his ears.

He was so not my type.

"You get good stuff at the thrift store?" He pulled a key out of his pocket and stuck it in the lock.

I shrugged. "Nothing great. But I guess I'll have to wear them. My dad packed the wrong clothes for me—nothing fits. And there's, like, no mall here or anything."

He pushed open the door.

"I'll probably just throw these out once I get my real clothes," I said.

He raised his eyebrows. "Those aren't real clothes?"

The first thing I saw when we walked into Leo and Delilah's apartment was a mirrored disco ball hanging from a string right inside the front door. As he walked under, Duncan jumped up and tapped it as if it were a basketball. It swung wildly from side to side, the little mirrors casting jewels of light around the walls.

"Holy crap," I said, looking up.

"Leo bought that," Duncan said.

"I kind of figured."

He grinned at the ceiling. "Only three bucks."

"Bargain."

"Leo throws dance parties up here." Duncan put his hands in his front pockets and looked at the ground. "Maybe you can come sometime."

"Sure." And maybe I can stick barbecue skewers in my eyes. I had a sudden vision of kids drinking apple juice out of NFL mugs while trading Pokémon cards. "But the thing is, I don't think I'll be in town very long."

He blinked at me. "Rose said you were moving here."

"What?" I shook my head. "I never said that! I'll be here for a little while—a few more weeks, maybe. But then I'm going home. I start school at the beginning of September."

"Oh," he said. "That's too bad." He sounded really disappointed. "But tonight? If you're not doing anything? A bunch of kids are going to have a bonfire out on the beach. Me and Leo and Delilah are going."

"I'll have to check with my parents," I said, thankful to be able to use them as an excuse. "Um, where's the bathroom?"

"Oh—right. It's over here." He led me across the little room, past a futon unfolded to create a bed (unmade), an old television on a fake-wood stand, and a cluttered bookshelf. There was a kitchenette only slightly less inadequate than the one at Home Suite Home. A small table and chairs, painted bright blue, sat under a tall window painted—what else?—purple.

Off the main room was one bedroom—or should I say, two almost bedrooms: a curtain ran along the center of the room. Each side had a single bed, the far one covered with a rumpled orange coverlet, the near with a crisp black one. The walls on the far, orange-bed side were yellow; on the black-bed side they were white and covered with colorful art. That side reminded me, in a weird way, of my room back home, which I'd decorated as a kind of mini photograph gallery.

"Bathroom's on Delilah's side," Duncan said, pointing to yet another little door on the white wall.

"But what happens when she's in here and someone has to use the bathroom?"

He shrugged as if it was obvious. "Then they walk through her room."

"But what about privacy?" I asked.

He shook his head, confused.

I took a step into the bathroom. "I'll meet you downstairs."

"You want me to wait for you?" He looked eager. Too eager.

"No, thanks. I can handle it."

* * *

The blue jeans were too short, while the black jeans were so baggy, they wouldn't even stay up. The white shirt had a tear in the seam, and the black shirt was loose around the shoulders. I should have let the zebra girl have it.

I wished I had attacked the merchandise like Delilah, grabbing everything in my path, figuring out what worked later. Tears pricked my eyes. I swallowed a lump of anger. How could my parents do this to me?

I put on the too-short blue jeans and the purple shirt and stuffed everything else into my plastic grocery bag. In the living room, the spray of light-jewels from the disco ball stopped me. The light sprinkled the pale yellow wall and danced across the futon's rumbled white sheets. I pulled out my camera and took a few shots: close-ups of the ball, tiny squares of light on the bright blue table. I snapped a picture of the window because I'd never seen one painted purple, the sill a bright green.

When I got back downstairs, they had cleared a spot in the room and tacked a pale blue sheet to the wall like a canvas. Another blue sheet lay on the floor below it. Delilah fussed with the dressmaker's dummy, adjusting a frilly white dress that I couldn't imagine her wearing. A digital camera on a tripod faced the dummy. Was that what all of this junk was about—Delilah's art?

When he saw me, Duncan popped up from the couch. "You look nice."

"The pants are too short," I said. I've never been good at taking compliments, even when they were deserved. And I wasn't used to compliments from a boy. But most of all, I felt stupid in the pants, which ended just above my ankles.

Delilah looked up from straightening the dress. "They'll make good cutoffs. There are some scissors on the table over there."

Suddenly, I felt better. She was absolutely right. I needed shorts more than jeans anyway. If I hadn't been so miserable, I would have thought of cutoffs myself.

"The black ones are way too baggy," I said, retrieving the scissors. "And the black shirt doesn't fit, either."

"So we'll sell them," Delilah said with a shrug. She went behind the tripod and peered into the camera lens. When she released the shutter, a flash seared the room. She checked the shot and then strode over to strip the dummy.

"We'll *what?*" I said.

"Sell them." She pulled the dress off the dummy, folded it carefully, and put it on a pile of clothes. Then she took a red T-shirt— *my* T-shirt—and spread it on the blue sheet on the ground. "We got any more Abercrombie in the same size?" she asked Leo.

"I'll check." He dug through a cardboard box till he found a cute yellow shirt.

Delilah laid the yellow shirt next to my red one, unscrewed the camera from the tripod, and snapped a picture.

"I'm confused," I admitted.

"We sell this stuff on eBay," Duncan told me, smiling. (Did he smile this much at everyone?)

"Brand names net the highest prices," Delilah said, folding up the Abercrombie shirts and adding them to the pile. "People are such sheep."

"Delilah hits the thrift store," Duncan said. "Leo and I do the yard sales."

"So you don't really collect Pokémon cards?" I asked.

He laughed. "Is that what you thought?"

I rolled my eyes. "Of course not."

"He's gaga for snow globes, though," Leo said.

"Shut up," Duncan said, turning red. "At least it's better than that crappy disco music you buy."

When Delilah finished photographing the clothes, she moved on to the mugs, shot glasses, and Pokémon cards. Meanwhile, I went back upstairs and turned my "new" jeans into "new" shorts. Then Delilah downloaded her shots onto the computer in the front of the shop. She frowned in concentration at the screen, picking just the right words for the ads.

At eleven o'clock, Leo unlocked the front door. "So, Dee, me and Duncan were thinking about skating down to the beach." He snuck one sneaker-clad foot onto the outside pavement.

"Duncan and I." Delilah's head shot up. "It's your day to watch the store."

He licked his lips. "Yeah, but you're busy with the computer right now, plus this is a really good opportunity for you to work on your art. . . ."

She frowned at him.

"I can't go to the beach, anyway," Duncan said. "My dad's boat is getting in now. I told him I'd meet him on the pier to clean fish." He looked at me. "You want to come with me? To ask him about that weird picture?"

"Sure." It's not like I had any other plans.

"Can I see it again?" Duncan asked.

I had a feeling he was just using that as an excuse to stand near me. For some reason that was okay.

I fished the camera out of its case and turned it on. The picture of Leo's disco ball came to life. "I just thought it might be a cool picture," I murmured, hurrying past it and the next shot, of the blue kitchen table sprinkled with light. I hoped they wouldn't think it was strange, me taking pictures of their apartment.

And then I got to the window shot: the purple trim, the green sill, the dirty panes.

I screamed.

Delilah bolted away from her computer and across the floor. I thrust the camera at her as if it were something frightening and alive.

The photo was supposed to be a still-life shot: objects only, nothing animate. But looking through the panes, staring straight at me, was a man.

Delilah's already pale face grew even whiter. "That's our window."

"I liked the colors," I croaked, embarrassment pushing past my terror.

"There's no roof or ledge outside that window," she whispered. "Nothing to stand on."

"There was no one there," I said.

The man had sandy-colored hair. His eyes were wide with happy surprise, his hands pressed against the windowpane. He was much younger than the old woman on the beach, closer to Rose's age than my parents'.

"Give me the memory card," Delilah said, pointing to my camera. "Let's see what it looks like on the big screen. Maybe it's just a shadow or something."

I popped the card out of my camera, and she slipped it into the photo printer. I didn't even realize I was holding my breath until Delilah pushed a few buttons and the photo loomed on the screen. The man's face was unmistakable, his expression oddly sweet, like he was looking at a kitten bounding after a ball, not peering through a second-floor window.

Leo stopped sneaking out the front door and came to get a closer look. "Mom always said this place had good energy, but she never said it was haunted."

"Mom wouldn't know if it was haunted," Delilah said, irritation tingeing the fear in her voice. "Besides, doesn't this guy look vaguely familiar?"

Leo checked the screen. "No."

"He does," I said, shuddering. How could that be? I'd only been here a week.

"I wouldn't know if what was haunted?" Rose asked, coming through the front door. Today she wore a cutoff jean miniskirt and the same black halter top I'd seen on her the last time. Her auburn hair hung loose around her shoulders.

Delilah pointed at the photo printer's screen. "Madison took this picture a little while ago. She swears there was no one in the window."

I expected Rose to start spouting stuff about ghosts and energy and transformation. Instead, she squinted at the screen and said, "Are you sure?"

I nodded.

She bit her lip. "Because sometimes the light hits the window in a funny way, and you can't see what's on the other side."

"There was no one there," I said.

"There's nothing to stand on," Delilah said.

Rose turned away from the printer. "Maybe he had a ladder.

The building next door is a bed-and-breakfast. Maybe it was a repairman."

"He wasn't there when I took the picture," I insisted.

"Leo thinks it's a ghost," Duncan said.

"There's no such thing as ghosts," Delilah said. "Besides, I keep feeling like I've seen this guy before. Do you recognize him, Mom?"

"No." Rose glanced at the screen. "But it's not a ghost."

"How do you know?" Duncan asked.

"That's not what ghosts look like."

Suddenly the room felt very, very cold. I hugged myself to keep from shivering.

Kimberley Cove, down from Sandyland Beach on the other side of the rock outcropping, was smaller than I expected, given that Duncan had told me it was the place where all the fishing boats moored. It was just a protected inlet with maybe thirty moorings, about half of which had boats attached. The pier that Duncan had mentioned was so small and weathered that most people would call it a dock. There was also a tiny unhygienic-looking clam shack and an even tinier building with a sign that said HAR-BORMASTER. Still, it was a pretty spot. The blue water, calmer than the open ocean, glinted with sequins of light. Some morning, I'd come back with my camera.

"There's my dad." Duncan waved, and a figure in a bright blue polo shirt waved back. He looked too preppy to be Larry, but as we got closer, I recognized the friendly smile and the puppy-dog eyes, the stubble and the cross dangling from one ear. The shirt was just a uniform.

Larry stood on the float at the end of the pier helping sun-burned men in T-shirts unload their gear from an unsteady-looking white boat. Inside the boat was another man, tall with steel-colored hair, wearing a matching bright blue polo. The boat, called the *Peggy*, had six seats on the open back deck and a raised bridge with a steering wheel. The bridge was so high, I got queasy just looking at it.

"Your dad's boat is smaller than I expected," I said (smooth as always).

"It's not a commercial fishing boat; it's a charter. Tourists pay to go out. And it's not my dad's boat. Captain's this guy named Ray Clarke."

"You ever go up on the bridge?" I asked, looking up.

"Oh, yeah—it's awesome. Best way to spot the fish." He held up an arm and pointed to the tips of his fingers, indicating the bridge. "And when you hit a wave?" He moved his arm, his fingers swooping around like a crazy bird. "It's like being on a roller coaster or something, only better because you're not strapped in. Total head rush."

Down at the float, Duncan got to work cleaning fish. "If you want, we could go to the beach when I'm done," he said.

"Thanks." I tried not to look at the fish guts. "But I need to stop by the Internet café to check my e-mail, and then I told my parents that I'd do something with them this afternoon."

Okay, that was a lame excuse, even if my parents weren't at work. But for now, at least, I just wanted to hang with Duncan in a group setting—you know, with my very temporary summer friends.

When Larry had finished unloading all of the tourists' gear, I pulled out my camera.

"Been working okay for you?" he asked.

"Yeah," I said. "It's just . . . Did Duncan tell you about the old woman who showed up in one shot?"

"Yeah," he said. "Weird."

"Well, there's this other picture I took today, over at . . . the apartment." (What was I supposed to call it? Delilah's house? Rose's?)

When he saw the window picture, he drew a sharp breath. "I told Rose to keep the shades down. I changed all the window locks—half of 'em were broken—but most of the time she just leaves the windows wide open." He looked up from the screen. "Did anyone call the cops?"

I shook my head. "The thing is, the guy wasn't there when I took the picture. Leo thinks he's a ghost." (That was easier to say than "I think he's a ghost.")

Larry stared at me, expressionless.

"Is it possible for the camera to do that? Take pictures of ghosts?"

He continued to stare. I squirmed with embarrassment.

"I don't actually believe in ghosts," I said, trying to cover myself. "I'm just trying to figure out what's going on."

His face relaxed. "There's plenty of stuff I don't understand. And, yeah, okay, maybe some people really are, whatever—extra sensitive. And maybe they can feel things the rest of us can't. I'm working real hard on that keep-an-open-mind deal, but ghosts—that's pushing it." I had a feeling he'd had this conversation with Rose one or twenty times.

"I'm with you," I said. "Totally." I didn't want to believe in ghosts. Ghosts scared me. *Get out of the house.*

88

"I'm just looking for an explanation," I continued. "Something technical, you know? The thing is, I'm positive that guy wasn't there. Can you get a double exposure on a digital camera?"

"No."

"Maybe?"

"No. Like I told you, the camera captures the light, stores the energy, and then translates it into a number. You can Photoshop an image on your computer, but it's not going to change in the camera."

"I'm sure he wasn't there," I said.

"Soon as I get out of here, I'm going to check those locks," he said. "Did you print this out?"

I shook my head.

"Maybe next time you're in the shop, then. I want to get a better look at this guy."

11.

THE INTERNET CAFÉ WAS PACKED. I had to hang out with my vanilla iced latte for almost an hour before I scored a computer. Whatever. It's not like I had anything better to do. I didn't want to go to the beach alone—and it would be really embarrassing if I ran into Duncan after saying I had plans with my parents. Photography was out because it would be hours before the sun fell low enough for any decent pictures—and besides, my camera was starting to give me the creeps.

"So I'll see you tonight," Duncan had said when I'd left him on the boat, up to his arms in fish guts. "At the bonfire."

"What time?" I asked, still not sure I wanted to go—and not sure my parents would let me.

"Nine o'clock?" he said. "I could come get you."

"No!" My parents would take one look at Duncan, with his crazy hair, his skater-boy clothes, and his earrings and—oh God. "My motel is kind of far." *And this is not a date.* "I'll just meet all of you in front of the shop."

When a computer finally opened up in the café, I dashed over with my cup of sweet, watery ice, having long since finished the latte. I went to MySpace. My home page popped up, the picture of me with brown hair seeming like yet another photo of a ghost.

There were more weird comments like the ones I'd seen before:

r u moving???

I'd almost asked my parents about the phone bill that morning, but I'd chickened out, not sure I was ready to hear what they had to say. Even though my mom was so totally in love with the house, it kind of made sense that they'd sell. After all, it was a really nice place; it would bring in a lot of money. Still, I hated the idea of moving into something smaller, giving up my room and the swimming pool.

Is that why they hadn't told me what was going on—because they knew I'd be upset? Maybe they were afraid I'd make a scene, but I wouldn't: tough times call for tough measures and all that. Besides, I reserved my scenes for occasions when they might actually do me some good.

Oh, well. Maybe they'd make enough money this summer to cover all of their payments.

Lexie had left me two messages. From Thursday:

where r u? u need a new cell! it rained @ the lake so we came back early.

The one from Friday—yesterday—read:

omg, mad, wd you call or i.m. or something??? saw
rolf last nt & all he cld talk about was u!!!!

The thought of Rolf made my hands shake. I wrote:

i'm still stuck @ the beach. can't w8t 2 leave. what
did rolf say???

Just as I hit "send," Lexie appeared online. Before I knew it,
we were IMing.

LEX: OMG! she lives! where r u???? ppl are saying
ur in the witness protection program.
MAD: LOL. sorry, nothing so exciting—just
sandyland.
LEX: when r u coming home?
MAD: not till aug, i think. where did u c rolf?
LEX: melissa's house. she had a few ppl over last
nt. rolf is on the paper too, doing special events or
sports or something random. anyway, he kept saying,
where's madison? so I go, y do u care? ur w/ celia?
MAD: OMG!!!! but u knew they broke up.
LEX: i wanted 2 hear wot he wd say. he goes, celia
was a mistake.
MAD: GET OUT!!!!!!
LEX: & he sd, i was kinda immature last yr & i
didn't no wot i wanted. and then he goes AGAIN,
where's madison? he's supposed 2 call me 2nt 2
talk about u.

At that, my Internet time ran out. I went to the counter to buy some more time, but the line was so long that by the time I logged on again, Lexie was gone. She'd left me a message, though.

dude! get a decent connection, ok?
anyways, rolf never came rt out 2 say he liked u, but
it was so totally obvious. he wanted 2 no when you'd
be back, AND he asked if u were dating anyone. ha!
i think u shd let him think u like him & then dump
him. let him c how it feels.
when r u coming back? my mom sd u cd sleep over.

A sleepover at Lexie's: that's what I needed. My dad was going back to get some stuff the next week—maybe I could go with him.

When I got back to Home Suite Home, my dad, his T-shirt filthy and sweat-soaked, was sitting on the brown bed, watching a juicer infomercial on TV.

"My friend Delilah asked me to hang with her tonight." I had to raise my voice to be heard over the television. "Okay?"

He shrugged and kept staring at the screen as a perky blond woman dropped apples and grapes into the juicer. If my parents found me in that kind of a trance, they'd accuse me of being on drugs.

"Is that a yes?" I asked.

He sighed. "Sure."

I still wasn't sure how I felt about Duncan, but anything was better than another night in that musty brown room. Besides,

after talking to Larry, I really wanted to print that window picture. I'd print the old lady on the beach, too. Maybe then things
would start to make sense.

But—did I really want them to make sense? Although it still
frightened me, I was warming to the idea of my camera being able
to capture ghosts. It was like having a superpower.

When my mom came home, I was busy deciding what to wear.
Should I go with the purple shirt and cutoff jean shorts? Or would
I look better wearing the cutoff jean shorts and the purple shirt?
Oh, I crack myself up.

"I went to the Laundromat after work," my mother told me,
sitting on the couch (my couch) and sticking her feet on the
coffee table. She had on black pants and a green polo shirt.
She'd forgotten to take off her nametag, which said CHERIE. Her
name is Linda. "Your big orange T-shirt is clean; I put it in your
drawer."

"You did laundry?" I said. "Without my clothes?"

She pulled a foot to her and rubbed it. "I couldn't wash your
clothes because you were wearing them." She blinked at me.
"Those new?"

"New to me," I said. "I went to the thrift shop today, remember? The shirt cost two dollars."

If that horrified her, she didn't let it show.

"I'm going to hang with my friend Delilah tonight," I said
casually.

That got her attention. "Who?"

"Delilah. I met her at the photo shop. She's an artist." Before
my mother could protest, I added, "Dad said I could go."

94

She glanced at my father on the bed and then she looked at me.

"Is she a nice girl?" she asked.

"No," I snapped. "She's a total bitch. That's why I want to hang out with her."

I don't know which one of us was more surprised by my outburst. What caused it: the sudden poverty? The black hair? In a schizophrenic attempt to make nice I chirped, "How was work?"

"We got in a huge bunch of yellow daisies," she said.

"Cool."

"I hate yellow daisies."

12.

As I walked toward Psychic Photo to meet Duncan—and Delilah and Leo (*this is not a date*)—all I could think about was Rolf Reinhardt and what a jerk he was and how I still kind of liked him.

Rolf had been in my ninth-grade honors English class. He was in choir with me, too, plus he ran track, which meant I saw him running around town every once in a while. He had nice legs. I got to know him when we staged an English class production of *Romeo and Juliet*. Rolf was Romeo, and I was—you guessed it: Romeo's mother. It could have been worse. The class had too many girls, and Lexie got stuck playing a nobleman. She had to wear yellow tights and this puffy purple hat with a feather. Celia Weaver played Juliet's father. I was really impressed with her performance. She was totally believable as a guy.

Can I just say? Rolf wasn't that cute. And he came after me, not vice versa.

Okay, he was kind of cute. He was really tall and skinny but with this baby face, chubby cheeks and all. Hair: brownish blond. Eyes: bluish gray. He wore jeans pretty much every day, along with layered polo shirts. Sometimes he'd wear three polos at once. At first I thought that was one too many, but the look grew on me.

Because of my role in the play, he started joking around with me.

Rolf: Hey, hot mama.

Madison: Don't you be a bad boy.

Rolf: But I'm good when I'm bad.

It was funny at the time. Or—it was something. It was flirting, clearly, and not like when I was younger. This was high school flirting. It meant something. We could go on an actual date, if only he'd ask me.

I wasn't the only one who noticed.

"Are you and Rolf going out?" Celia asked me in the hall one day. Celia was half a head taller than me, with long blond hair. That sounds good, but she wasn't that pretty because her hair was stringy and her nose had this funky bulb on the end. Plus, she hardly ever smiled, and when she did, it looked fake.

I widened my eyes in mock confusion. "Me and Rolf? No! Why?"

She tightened her already thin lips. "Someone just said something."

"Who?"

"I don't remember."

Celia was one of those hypercompetitive people who always had to be the best at everything. She was famous for convincing teachers to change her B's to A's, for elbowing other players on the soccer field, and for arranging second-chance auditions for choir solos, claiming she had undiagnosed strep throat the first time around.

Rolf finally asked me out on a date—well, me and twenty-six other people. On the day of our performance (we put on a lame show for three other English classes, who didn't care that we sucked because they got out of class), he asked the entire honors English group to his house for a cast party after school. His mother was there-but-not-there. She said hello at the beginning—you know, just to discourage us from drinking beer, smoking pot, taking off our clothes, or doing anything else that we had all read about but never actually done—and then she faded away.

We hung out in Rolf's media room, which had this mongo plushy beige couch and a television screen that took up most of the wall. There was a mini drinks fridge filled with fizzy juices (Rolf's mom didn't believe in soda). Someone turned on a movie, and Rolf dimmed the lights. The room had tiny windows and blackout shades, which made it look like night.

He took my hand and pulled me over to the couch. We settled in and watched the movie, holding hands. The movie was all car chases and robots and explosions. Not that it mattered. All I could think about was Rolf and his hand. He had this thing he did, rubbing his thumb against my palm, which was borderline annoying but also cool. It felt like Morse code for "I like you."

Eventually, he whispered, "Save my seat," his breath hot on my ear. He got us a couple of fizzy juices—one mango, one apricot-lime—and asked me which I preferred (mango). Then he sat back down and put his arm around me. I snuggled into him, not even bothering to finish my mango fizz, which really didn't taste all that good.

People were watching us. They were pretending not to, but I

could tell. Farther down the couch this other couple was sucking face, but they'd been going out for almost a year, so no one really cared.

After the movie, everyone whipped out cell phones to call their parents. Rolf, his arm still around me, whispered, "Stay a little longer." We remained planted on the couch, clearly a couple, waving our lazy good-byes. Lexie snuck me a wink. Celia didn't even look at us.

When everyone had gone, Rolf made his move. He held my face with both his hands and went in for the kill. I put my arms around his neck. Our teeth clinked. We readjusted.

His lips were surprisingly soft. I would have expected a guy's lips to be chapped or something. He smelled good, like laundry softener. His mouth tasted like apricot mixed with artificial lime. He pushed a little harder against my mouth than was strictly necessary, and I kept wishing he'd move his hands from my face to my back, but mostly it was nice for my first real kiss. And besides, we'd have plenty of time to work on our technique. We were just getting started.

After maybe fifteen minutes, his mother walked in. Total mortification. She covered her mouth to (sort of) hide her smile and said, "Sorry, kids—don't let me interrupt." Then she gave us a little wave and backed out the door.

Talk about a mood killer.

I stood up. "I should probably go." And then, just to make sure he knew I liked him, I added, "We can continue this later."

He stood up, said, "Yeah. Definitely," and kissed me one last time. He said he had plans all weekend, but he'd see me Monday. And then he programmed my number into his cell, which clearly signaled a committed relationship.

I told Lexie all about it, of course, the instant I got home. With my permission, she called a couple of other people, who e-mailed a whole bunch more. By Monday, everyone in honors English knew we were a couple.

Celia certainly knew. She kept huddling with her friends, arms crossed, and glaring at me across various classrooms. There was nothing going on between her and Rolf at that point, so she had no right to hate me.

That week, Rolf and I talked twice on the phone (I still had my cell), texted daily, and IMed once. News of our couple status reached choir. I told my mother that I had a boyfriend. She sat me down for a talk about adolescent urges that I'd rather not revisit at this point.

He never officially asked me out—which is just one of many reasons why I was so pissed when he dumped me a week later. The kiss-off speech: "I really like you, but I'm so focused on my school-work and track and choir and stuff, I just don't have time for a relationship right now. Plus, my mom was talking about signing me up for an SAT prep course, so I'm going to be really busy."

An SAT prep course, my ass. We were freshmen.

Within the month, he managed to find time for a relation-ship—with Celia. I wasn't brokenhearted, really, just humiliated. Plus, I always had this weird suspicion that Celia never noticed Rolf until Rolf noticed me.

Since then, it had been my dream to win Rolf back from Celia, to have him gaze into my eyes, build his world around me—and then to dump him on his butt.

I am the last of the great romantics.

13.

WHEN I SHOWED UP AT NINE O'CLOCK, Duncan was sitting on the
bench in front of Psychic Photo. At the sight of me, he jumped
up and smoothed his jeans and then his hair, which was damp
from the shower and curling at the whitish blond ends. He looked
good, I had to admit, his chocolate brown hoodie the same color
as his hair.

"Hey, G.G. You look pretty," he blurted.

I studied the ground. "I look the same as I did this afternoon."

"You looked pretty this afternoon, too."

I cleared my throat. "I was thinking maybe I could print out
those photos. You know, of the man in the window and the old
lady on the beach."

He glanced at the darkened building. "The shop's locked. But
I can meet you here in the morning."

I looked around for Delilah and Leo. "Where is everyone?"

Duncan slid his hands into the front pockets of his jeans. "At
the beach already."

For an instant I felt hurt that Delilah would leave without me. And then I got it. She'd set me up.

This is not a date.

I crossed my arms in front of my purple chest. I wasn't just being defensive; it was getting cold. "Let's go find them, then."

I half expected Duncan to pull out his skateboard and whiz down the street, but he kept pace with me as we walked, his beat-up Vans quiet on the sidewalk. Downtown was practically deserted The shops were dark, and only one almost-empty restaurant was still open.

Soon we could hear the ocean, the waves gentler than during the day, their breaks a hiss rather than a crash. The air was damp and salty. On one side of the road, streetlights lit a deserted park. Our silence grew uncomfortable.

"What's your real name?" I blurted. I'd been wondering about it more than I cared to admit.

He waited a moment before answering. "Can't tell you."

"Can't or won't?"

He considered. "Won't."

Now I was really curious.

We continued down the street, the ocean sounds growing louder with every step.

"Adam?" I tried, beginning at the beginning.

He looked at me in surprise, and then he grinned. "No."

"Andrew? Alex?"

"No."

Above us, the stars looked like pinpricks of light. They were a lot brighter here than they were in Amerige.

After a few more A names I moved on to the Bs. "Brian, Brett,

Brandon, Billy, Bob, Boris, Blaine, Blair, Bo . . ."

"Byron," he said.

"That's your name?"

"No. But it seemed like you should have tried it." He threw his head back and laughed. I smacked him on the arm and laughed along with him, forgetting to think about whether or not this was a date.

When we reached the beach, I pulled off my orange flip-flops. The bonfire glowed in the distance. As we walked across the cold, coarse sand, I worked my way through the alphabet. He said, no, no, no—though he admitted to calling himself Frankie for a short time when he was twelve "because I really like hot dogs."

We were almost at the bonfire when I reached the Rs. "Tell me your name's not Rolf."

He scrunched up his nose. "You mean Ralph?"

I hugged myself tight. The closer we got to the ocean, the colder it became. "No, Rolf."

"Is that really a name? It sounds like an animal sound—you know, a kitty cat says, 'Meow,' and a dog says, '*Rolf!*'" He put his hands up like a begging dog and began to pant.

The idea of Rolf begging anyone for anything made me laugh.

Duncan took off his brown hoodie and pressed it against my crossed arms. "You're cold." His teeth gleamed in the moonlight.

"But if I wear this, you'll be cold."

"I'll warm up at the fire."

I pulled the sweatshirt over my head. He took my hand and pulled me to the circle of light. I had about a minute, maybe less, of thinking how good it all felt: the warmth of Duncan's sweatshirt, the feel of his hand. And then I got a look at the crowd around the bonfire. I didn't see Delilah and Leo right away, just a bunch of normal-looking people. Instead of thrift shop rags, they wore Hollister, Abercrombie, Aeropostale, American Eagle—all the regular brands. They looked like my crowd from home: the good kids. There were people in Sandyland just like me. What was I doing with Duncan and Delilah and Leo?

Summer friends. That's what they were. It was just temporary. I still had my real friends at home.

"Hey, Duncan." A girl came out of the shadows. She was super-skinny, with blond hair dried straight and the brand of jeans that I had spent much of ninth grade (unsuccessfully) begging my mother to buy me. She flashed Duncan a full-metal smile, and self-satisfaction washed over me; I'd gotten my braces off in eighth grade.

"Hey, Ricki, whassup?" Duncan said, being nice. Too nice?

"Just, you know, hanging." She tucked a strand of overtreated hair behind her ear. She had a single gold ball in each lobe.

"This is Madison," he told Ricki, squeezing my hand.

Her eyes narrowed, and she gave me a once-over. Suddenly, I saw myself through her eyes. Here I'd been feeling funny about hanging around with Duncan, when he had every right to feel embarrassed about being seen with me, a girl with dull black hair and secondhand clothes.

Ricki turned her attention back to Duncan. "You going anywhere this summer?"

"Nah, just hanging." He put his arm around me, which shouldn't have surprised me but did. What surprised me even more was that I liked it.

104

At this, she was forced to acknowledge me. "You just here for the summer?"

I shrugged. "I guess." I slid my arm around Duncan's waist.

Her mouth and eyes tightened, and then she bared her teeth in a shiny almost-smile. "See you in September, Duncan." She wandered away.

"Ex-girlfriend?" I asked once she was out of earshot.

"Who, Ricki?" Duncan sounded genuinely surprised. "No, just someone I know from school. Why would you say that?"

"No reason," I said, an image of Celia flashing through my mind.

It took a few minutes to find Delilah and Leo, surrounded by a mob. Fear shot through my stomach. What was going on? Was someone hurting them? But Duncan didn't look nervous, and as we got closer, I could hear the voices:

"You gotta do this!"

"Please? You're the only one."

"I saw it. I swear."

"Just for a minute—before it's too late!"

"Hey, guys!" Delilah pushed herself up from the sand. She was dressed kind of normally, in denim overalls and a T-shirt. Her red faux-fur jacket was pure Delilah, though.

"What's the deal?" Duncan asked. The crowd—there must have been ten or twelve people at least—spoke at once:

"Down by the point—"

"Something weird, didn't really get a good look—"

"This funky light, kind of greenish white and glowing—"

"A ghost!"

"They want me to do a séance," Delilah said, totally casually,

105

like she was saying, "They want me to help them with their algebra."

"Do you . . . do those?" I asked. Maybe Rose wasn't the only psychic in her family.

Delilah's eyes shot from side to side. "Not anymore. I'm not comfortable with what I might stir up." Around her, the kids grew silent. "But I'll walk down the beach, see if I sense anything."

I began to shiver, from fear more than cold. Duncan squeezed my shoulders. "We'll come with you," he said.

Other kids wanted to join us, but Delilah said no: too many people would frighten the spirit away. Leo, wearing white slacks and a Hawaiian shirt, completed the expedition. His presence made me feel better, as if his essential goofiness was a kind of foil against anything frightening or evil.

We trudged along in silence for a few moments. Duncan and I held hands; by then it felt natural. Delilah kept her hands in the pockets of her fuzzy jacket, while Leo hunted the ground for flat rocks, which he flung into the water, cheering when they skipped along the surface.

"Four!" he'd announce, counting the skips. Or, "Eleven! New record!"

My eyes darted around, expecting to see a ghost at every corner, but all I saw was darkness, a hint of phosphorescence in the waves, the odd beam of light from the enormous homes looming above the rock wall.

Finally, Duncan spoke. "You said you weren't going to do this anymore."

"They didn't give me much choice," Delilah said. "And anyway, I refused to do the séance."

"But you used to do them?" I asked. No wonder she'd been so casual about the figures in my photographs: ghosts were no big deal to her.

"Not that much," she said. "Just a few times in eighth grade. Mostly I read minds and told futures."

"You read minds?"

"Oh, sure." She stopped walking and studied me. "Let's see . . . you're worried about what people think of your hair and your clothes."

My stomach began to hurt.

"And you like Duncan."

My face grew hot.

"But you're not sure where things with him are going to lead."

My knees grew wobbly. I had a sudden urge to flee, to get as far away from Delilah as possible. What else did she know about me?

When she saw my expression, Delilah laughed.

"You suck," Duncan told her.

"Can you see my future?" I asked, unsure if I wanted to know.

"Oh my God," Leo said, rubbing a flat rock between his fingers.

"Tell her," Duncan commanded, with an edge I'd never heard before.

"Sorry, Madison, I was kidding," Delilah said. "I thought you realized."

I shook my head with confusion. Out beyond the waves the moon shone fuzzy white, a fog blurring the edges.

"I'm just good at reading people—you know, their expressions and body language," Delilah admitted. "But I can't read minds. Or communicate with ghosts."

"Or tell the future," Leo added.

"And you can't read palms, either," Duncan said.

She pointed her index finger at him. "Now there you're wrong. Anyone can read palms. You just have to know which line is which."

Back at the wide public beach, the bonfire glowed orange. Ahead of us, there was darkness, rocks, churning surf. And Delilah couldn't see anything supernatural. But could my camera?

"Why did you pretend, then?" I was pretty annoyed. "They all think you're psychic."

She crossed her arms. "Bunch of sheep. They'll believe anything. You can't imagine how often they send me on these ridiculous ghost hunts. Someone in a beach house walks near the rocks with a flashlight, and all of a sudden it's a message from beyond."

"Cats," Leo said.

"Oh, yeah," Delilah said. "I get sent after cats a lot: the glowing eyes, the rustling in the trees. Raccoons, too. Those are *really* scary."

"So—those people aren't your friends?" I thought of all the people crowding around Delilah at the bonfire. Was she really that fake?

Delilah sighed. She wandered over to the rock wall and pulled herself up, settling down next to a KEEP OFF ROCKS sign. The three of us followed and arranged ourselves on the boulders like barnacles. Duncan sat just above me and to the side, stroking my hair.

"Sixth grade was a tough year," Delilah said, finally. "That's when we moved onto Main Street and opened the shop. Before that, my mom just worked out of our apartment, calling herself a spiritual healer. For some reason, that was okay—New Agey but not full-out weird, you know? I was always kind of different, I guess, but until then, the other kids didn't seem to notice."

The fog held us in a kind of cocoon. The waves hissed gently. I forgot, for the moment, about ghosts.

Leo broke the silence. "Everyone thought I was different right from the start."

Our laughter was a relief.

"Kids can be mean," Delilah said, her voice cracking a little. "Some of them said my mother was a witch. Others said she was a fake. Nobody wanted to eat lunch with me or even be seen with me. They made fun of me and my mother and—" She stopped dead.

"It doesn't bother me," Leo said. "Really." He wasn't entirely convincing.

Delilah found a loose pebble among the boulders and flung it out to sea, but we didn't hear it land.

"The summer between sixth and seventh grades, I tried to convince my mother to homeschool me," Delilah said. "She refused."

Leo snorted. "You'd be better off homeschooling her."

Delilah said, "But she said the most amazing thing: 'They're just saying that stuff because they feel bad about themselves.' It was total crap, of course, but it gave me an idea. On the first day of school the next year, this nasty girl named Avon said something inane about me casting spells or eating toads or something. I stared at her for, like, twenty seconds. And then I whispered,

'Oh, my God.'" Delilah covered her mouth and widened her eyes in mock horror.

"And she's all, 'What? What?'" she continued. "And I'm all, 'I can't tell you! Just—be careful.' She begged me to tell her what I'd seen, but I said I couldn't."

"Unless she coughed up some cash," Leo broke in.

Delilah sighed. "I didn't feel bad about taking her money. Such a poor excuse for humanity . . ."

"What did you tell her?" I asked.

"Nothing right away," Delilah said. "I tortured her for a couple of weeks. Every time I saw her, I stopped dead and stared. Then I'd hurry away like whatever I'd seen had frightened me."

"Brilliant," I said.

"Plus, I started doing it to a couple of other offenders," Delilah said. "And then the word spread, and the demand grew and . . ."

"She had a nice little business going," Leo said. "Not as good as the eBay stuff, but at least we didn't have to get up early on Saturday mornings for the yard sales."

"What did you tell that girl?" I asked. "What was it—Avon?"

Delilah smiled. "I said that something bad was going to happen to someone she loved—or maybe to someone close to someone she loved. I threw that in to cover my butt. I said I couldn't see the picture clearly, but I thought it was going to happen outdoors."

"Did it?" I asked.

"A month later, her cousin had a car accident."

"Oh, my God." That was kind of creepy.

Delilah made a little waving motion. "She was fine. And I'm not sure Avon even loved her. But it was enough to establish my reputation." She slid off the rock. We all followed, Duncan helping me down with both hands, being super-careful even though I was, like, two feet from the sand.

"Do you still tell fortunes?"

She shook her head. "I gave it up when I started high school because it was wrong—and also because I wasn't charging enough. I mean, five bucks a reading? Ridiculous."

"So you don't have any psychic abilities?" I pressed. "Because I've heard they can be genetic."

Delilah leveled her gaze. "Madison. Get real. No one has psychic abilities. My mom is a loon. There are rational explanations for all supernatural phenomena."

"What about ghosts?" I asked.

"No such thing," Delilah insisted, brushing a bit of sand off her overalls.

"But my photographs . . ." I said.

Delilah sighed. She sounded like an exasperated adult talking to an especially irritating two-year-old. It annoyed me.

"Just because we don't understand something doesn't mean it's supernatural," Delilah said. "That's the kind of thinking that once made people believe in rain gods and the man in the moon."

We were quiet for a moment. Duncan squeezed my hand. I didn't squeeze back. I wanted Lexie. I wanted to go home.

Leo tapped his chin, thinking. "The figures in Madison's photos have to be ghosts. It's the only thing that makes any sense."

Delilah said, "Ugh," and rolled her eyes.

"They could be," Duncan added.

"Sure," Delilah said. "And I'm the Easter bunny."

"Guess that explains the fuzzy coat," I said.

Delilah's mouth dropped open. I wished I could undo my words; Delilah wasn't the kind of person you talked back to. But after a moment she smiled. "Hey, Leo, let's walk back to the fire. I'm getting kind of cold."

"So what's their deal?" I asked Duncan. We were at the end of the beach, where the rocks jutted into the ocean, just past the point where I'd taken the first creepy photograph.

We took a few steps into the ocean. Foamy water scurried around our bare feet. Duncan had told me that stingrays swam out here during the day, but he was pretty sure they slept at night.

"Whose deal?" he asked. He'd rolled up his jeans, but the bottoms were getting splashed anyway.

"Delilah and Leo. And Rose. Especially Rose. How old is she?"

"Thirty-one next month," he said. "It's totally freaking her out that she can be that old. Rose is great, but she can be a real drama queen."

The numbers whirred through my brain. "So she had Leo when she was . . ."

"Fifteen," Duncan said. "Delilah says that's why Rose is, like, emotionally stuck. But that's just the kind of thing Delilah says because Delilah acts like she's forty. Rose is cool."

"What about their father?" I lifted my camera and snapped a random shot, as I'd been doing ever since Delilah and Leo had headed back to the bonfire. Duncan leaned over me, and we peered at the screen: no ghost.

"They don't talk about it. Though Rose mentioned something about bad chakras."

112

"And what about your dad?" I asked. "How are his chakras?" I pictured Larry with his heavy eyebrows and bandannas. He and Rose seemed like a really weird combination.

Duncan reached into the foam and pulled out a rock. He peered at it for a moment before tossing it far into the surf. It landed with a splash.

He said, "Rose says my dad's magnetic field is all screwed up, which is why he can't stay in one place. We've been in Sandyland over a year. That's a record."

"So you're staying?"

He stared into the distance. "Nah," he said finally. "I think we'll leave soon."

"Why?" Since I wouldn't be sticking around, either, that shouldn't have bothered me as much as it did.

"My dad's getting restless. He'd stay if Rose was more into him, but he's asked her to marry him, like, four times, and she won't commit." He snorted. "She says she's too young."

"How did they meet?" I asked.

"Rose was visiting a meditation center in this town where we were living. My dad was working at a convenience store, which he hated because he likes to work with his hands, but it was the only job he could find. Anyway, Rose came in for a cup of herbal tea. Three days later we moved here."

"Weren't you mad?" I asked. "I mean, having to leave your friends and stuff?"

He shrugged—just one shoulder, like it was no big deal. "We'd only been there a couple of months. I didn't have any friends."

"So . . . do you want to leave Sandyland?" I had to admit: tonight it seemed like a pretty nice place.

"No," he said simply. "I like it here. But—I kinda gotta go with whatever my father wants. He's the only family I've got."

He reached into the surf and pulled out a shell. He held it up to the moonlight and then handed it to me. "It's a sand dollar. For good luck."

I tucked the shell into the hoodie pocket. And then I aimed my camera toward the beach and snapped the darkness. We bent our heads over the screen. Half of me was afraid that another figure would appear, and the other half hoped that one would. But there was nothing there but water.

Nothing says romance like an overlit parking lot, an open-all-night McDonald's, and the haze of freeway fumes. Still holding hands, Duncan and I stood within view of Home Suite Home on a tiny patch of grass by the curb, in the shadow of a mangy-looking pine tree.

Duncan took my other hand and pulled me closer. He was only a couple of inches taller than me, which meant I could look straight into his eyes.

"Can I buy you a Big Mac?" he asked. The golden arches (the real ones, not my mother's eyebrows) glowed behind him.

I shook my head. It was almost midnight: my curfew back home. Did I have a curfew here? Did it matter?

"Then can I kiss you?" he asked.

The air between us felt electric. My stomach fluttered. Had I felt this nervous before Rolf had kissed me?

I held Duncan's gaze. I wanted to kiss him so much, but it felt like I should know him longer or better. I didn't even know his last name. Come to think of it, I didn't even know his *first* name.

"Tell me your real name. Then you can kiss me."

His mouth turned down at one corner. He frowned, thinking. Finally, he gave my hands a final squeeze—and dropped them. "Well, good night then."

"Good night?" This was not going the way I had planned it.

"I had fun."

"Oh." I crossed my arms over my chest and thought about how much boys suck.

He looked cold, standing there in the shadows. I yanked his sweatshirt over my head.

"You can give it to me tomorrow," he said. "When we print out your photos."

"I don't need it anymore." I rubbed the goose bumps on my arms.

He nodded once and yanked the sweatshirt over his head. "It smells like you."

"Sorry," I said.

"No, that's a good thing."

"Not always," I admitted.

He touched my cheek and put his hands in the front pocket of his hoodie before pulling out something round and white. "You almost forgot your sand dollar."

I took the shell. "Oh, yeah—for good luck." Fat lot of good it was doing me.

"I'll wait here," Duncan said. "Till you get inside."

"You don't have to." Across the parking lot, a faint light glowed in the window of my room.

"I want to," he said. "So, I'll see you at the shop tomorrow? It opens at ten. And by the way, my last name is Vaughn."

* * *

My parents were both awake, lying in bed with the light on. My mother turned her head when I opened the door.

"Did you have fun?" she asked quietly.

I shrugged. "It was okay." (He didn't kiss me.)

She was quiet for such a long moment, I thought she'd fallen asleep. "We're glad you're home," she said finally.

"This isn't home." It just popped out.

I walked toward the bathroom, but she stopped me just as I was about to turn on the light. "Madison, we have something to tell you."

14.

LOOKING BACK ON THAT MOMENT when I stood in the bathroom door is like seeing another girl. I thought I knew who I was: Madison Sabatini, fifteen years old. Lexie's best friend. The newest yearbook photographer. A shopaholic with cute accessories and great hair. Well, maybe not so much anymore.

I wish someone had taken my picture at that instant. I would have called the shot "Before."

My father stayed lying on the bed. "I'm sorry, Madison."

As a general rule, if someone says, "I'm sorry," for no apparent reason, you're screwed.

"Okay," I said, thinking, *Let's just get this over with.* Were they getting divorced after all?

My mother got out of bed and stood in the middle of the floor in her nightgown, arms crossed over her chest. She glared back at my father like she was waiting for him to say something—or at least open his eyes, which were closed now.

I'd live with my mother, of course. Weekend visits with my

dad. They wouldn't make me choose.

Finally, my mother spoke. "We lost the house."

At first, I didn't understand. "But it's just where we left it," I replied stupidly.

My mother shook her head. "Not that kind of lost. We have loans. A lot of them. For the house, the pool, the cars. We're six months behind on our mortgage. So now—the bank is taking the house."

I shook my head. She wasn't making any sense. And did this mean no divorce? "So ask the bank for a little more time."

"We did."

"But why don't you just sell the house? And then we can buy something smaller." I'd already kind of, sort of accepted that this might happen.

My father finally sat up in bed and opened his eyes, though he still wouldn't meet my gaze. "We can't sell. The real estate market has gone down since we bought the house. We owe more money on it than it's worth."

"What about your credit cards?" I asked, my stomach growing queasy. This couldn't be happening.

"They're already maxed out," my father admitted.

"But what about our things?" My voice cracked. Maybe this was all a big joke. Tell me it's a joke. Tell me they're getting divorced and this is their weird way of softening the blow.

"Most of the furniture, the TVs—they were all bought on credit," my father said, still gazing at nothing. "The stores sent trucks to our house last week. Picked everything up."

My mother cleared her throat. "Your father talked to the bank today. They're giving us one week to get everything else out. After that, the sheriff will change the locks. Your father is going back on Wednesday to move everything into a storage unit." She blinked: must have had something in her eye. Tears were out of the question.

She continued. "After that, the bank will auction off the house. The signs are probably out on our lawn already." Her voice cracked. With her two index fingers she wiped tears—they really were tears—from below her eyes.

The bank was going to auction off our house? My mind began to whirl. What else did that mean? How long would it take before things got back to normal? *How could they be so stupid?*

I held on to the doorjamb and tried to steady my breathing. I'd already considered the possibility of selling the house, but this just sucked. And it *was* kind of embarrassing. At school, I'd play it down. My mother was bored with the house. My father wanted to rent until the real estate market hit rock bottom.

"Why a storage unit?" I said. "I mean, we're going to have to rent another house anyway—might as well find something now."

My parents didn't answer. That's when it hit me.

"We are going home, aren't we?" Still nothing. *"Aren't we?"*

"I've spent months trying to drum up work," my father said.

"You've spent months watching TV in your bathrobe," I said, not caring that I hurt him.

"Nobody around us is building anymore," my mother said, her voice tight.

"So Dad can get a different kind of job."

"It's not that easy," my mother said.

"People are still building at the beach," my father said.

I pictured a sand castle.

119

My mother said, "There's money at the beach."

I imagined a quarter gleaming in the sand.

And then I got it. "We're moving to *Sandyland?*"

"We can get back on our feet here," my mother said, her voice back to its usual steadiness.

"I can't just leave my friends and my school!" I shouted. "How can you do this to me?"

If my camera had captured this moment, I would have deleted the shot immediately. And then I would have backed up to the picture I wished I could have taken before my parents had said anything: of me coming in from a night out with my summer boyfriend, with no real care in the world.

15.

WHEN I WOKE UP ON SUNDAY, about two hours later than usual, my mother said, "Do you want me to make you coffee?"

I nodded. My brain was still fuzzy with sleep but not muddled enough to convince me that last night's conversation had been a dream.

The room was oddly quiet: the TV was off. "Where's Dad?"

"Working."

"On a Sunday?"

"Just till noon. It was some kind of emergency. They're paying him double."

The gurgling coffee filled the silence between us. "You want me to pour you some cereal?" she asked finally.

"No," I said. My mother was trying to play nice, but I wasn't going to let her. Okay, except for the coffee, which I really needed.

Once it was ready, I took a mug and my camera out to the patio and shut the sliding door behind me. I closed my eyes and tried to think of nothing.

It didn't work. I thought about all of my friends from home. What would everyone say? How would I tell Lexie? And what about Rolf, who, according to Lexie, was so into me again? Not that I cared about Rolf anymore.

But there was Melissa Raffman and the newspaper—they still mattered. A lot. I remembered the day Melissa called to congratulate me. As soon as I got off the phone, I called Lexie, and we screamed and screamed because we were both on *The Buzz* staff, which meant our lives were going to be perfect.

My mother opened the slider. "We're going apartment hunting this afternoon."

I clutched my coffee mug. "Will we shoot to kill or just maim?"

She didn't think that was funny, and okay, maybe it wasn't, but you have to give a girl credit for trying.

"I'm going for a walk," she said. "If you go out, make sure you're back by noon." She closed the slider.

I reached for my camera and turned it on. I scrolled through the photographs until I reached the ones I'd taken of Lexie and her sisters on my last day in Amerige.

How could that life be gone if I could still see it glowing on the little screen? Larry had said that pixels capture energy. Didn't that mean that my world still existed, if only in a small way? I wished I could crawl into the camera, back into my old life.

Looking at the pictures made my chest hurt with sadness, so I flicked forward: nothing like a few ghosts to take your mind off things. There was the old lady on the beach. There was the young man in the window.

The shots from the night before showed moonlit waves and shadowy sand—nothing strange or spooky. If there had been ghosts on the beach with Duncan and me, my camera hadn't seen them.

For some reason, that made me feel even worse.

When I got to Psychic Photo, Duncan was sitting on the green bench outside the purple front door. When he saw me, he popped up and tucked his hair behind his ears. He was wearing the same thing he'd had on the first day I'd met him: long shorts and a black T-shirt. "Be careful," I said. "Some crazy-ass skateboarders hang out around here. They might run you down."

I almost hadn't come—but then I figured I could just as easily be miserable downtown as in my motel room. To my surprise, the misery drained away—at least temporarily—the moment Duncan flashed me a big smile.

God, he was cute—whatever his name was. I'd totally over-reacted the night before.

"You just get here?" I asked.

He shook his head. "My dad was afraid that the guy in the window would sneak in during the night, so we stayed over."

There was a motorcycle parked in the space right in front of us.

"But there was no guy in the window," I insisted. As long as I could concentrate on ghosts, I didn't have to think about the rest of my life.

Duncan nodded. "I know. And I said to my dad, 'No way do I want to sleep someplace haunted,' but he was all, 'I have to protect Rose.'" He rolled his eyes. "Sometimes I think my dad needs to be protected *from* Rose, but—whatever."

Inside the shop, Rose and Larry sat behind the counter, Rose sipping out of a chunky ceramic mug and Larry fiddling with some big electronic thing. They were such opposites, the tough biker

and the wispy psychic, but they seemed to go together somehow—like each one alone was too extreme but together they bal-
anced each other and made a normal couple.

Okay, maybe "normal" is an overstatement.

"Any luck?" Duncan asked Larry, pointing to the electronics.

Larry shook his head.

"It's a Wii," Duncan told me. "Got it at a yard sale for ten
bucks. Smokin' deal."

"Not if it doesn't work," I said.

"Larry will get it working." I'd never heard someone call his
father by his first name.

"You want a cup of green tea, Madison?" Rose asked. "Larry
can make you some."

"Um, no thanks."

Larry put down his screwdriver and wiped his hands on his
jeans. "You got the camera?"

I handed it to him. He slipped out the memory chip and stuck
it in the photo printer. Even though the initial shock had worn
off, it still freaked me out to see the man's face looming in the
window, lit up on the big screen.

"You sure you don't recognize him?" Larry asked Rose without
taking his eyes off the man's face.

"Positive."

"I'm going to print this out," he said. "Give it to the police."
His mouth in a hard line, he punched some instructions into the
machine.

"There's nothing the police can do," I said. "He wasn't there
when I took the picture."

Larry didn't respond, but Rose said, "I believe you," and Duncan

124

hooked his pinky around mine and murmured, "Me, too."

It wasn't until the photo had printed and I could see the shot without the computer screen's brightness that I noticed it.

"The man is shining," I said. "Like he's lit from within or something. Just like the old woman." A chill washed over me. I squeezed Duncan's pinky with my own.

"It's just a ray of sun," Larry said.

"It was overcast that day," I insisted.

"The sun could have come out for a minute," Larry countered.

"But it didn't. And anyway, if the sun hit him, there'd be shadows."

Before I could worry about how ridiculous the question might sound, I blurted, "Rose, what does a ghost look like?"

She gazed into the distance with her enormous pale eyes, utterly unsurprised by the question. "Like nothing."

"Huh?"

"A ghost doesn't have a body. You don't see it—you feel it. Like an energy field or a gust of cold air."

I shuddered.

"You said something about an old woman?" Rose asked, her voice calm and soothing. I'd bet anything it was the same tone she used with her clients.

"She was the first one to show up in my camera," I said. "In a shot down by the rocks. And I'm positive there was no one there."

"And she was shining as well?" Rose asked.

"This isn't about an old woman!" Larry burst out. "Or about lighting! Don't you get it, Rosie? Some sicko is spying on you. We've got to deal with it!"

Larry looked at Rose with such intensity: love mixed with sadness mixed with fear. Rose, meanwhile, just raised her eyebrows and sipped the tea that Larry had fixed for her. No wonder Larry was threatening to leave town. It couldn't be easy for him to be around her.

"The old woman's on the same memory chip, right?" Duncan asked.

At the printer, I zipped through my shots until I reached the picture.

"My first ghost," I said, trying to sound funny (and failing completely).

Rose put her tea on the counter and crossed the room to the printer. She leaned forward to get a better look. "That's not a ghost."

"Because she has a body?"

She shook her head. "Because I know her. She's one of my clients."

It took a moment for that to sink in. Something drained out of me, and I felt . . . disappointed? First I'd lost my house. Now I'd lost my superpower.

"I could have sworn I was alone," I whispered.

"Francine can be real quiet when she wants to be," Rose said. "Plus, she's pretty sick, so she can't move very fast."

Wait a minute. "Francine?"

"Yes, Francine Lunardi. We do our sessions at her house because it's hard for her to get around. I'm surprised she went all the way to the beach."

I suddenly felt very cold. "Francine Lunardi died," I croaked. "Delilah was supposed to tell you."

Rose began to blink. "Delilah doesn't even know her." Her voice sounded tense, not airy-fairy-psychic at all.

"Delilah talked to some lady at the thrift store yesterday. Mrs. Voorhees? She said that Mrs. Lunardi died on Friday."

Rose's huge eyes grew even wider. She covered her mouth.

Duncan touched the screen. "So she is a ghost. Which means the guy is, too."

"There's no such things as ghosts!"

We all turned to face Larry, still stationed by the printer, fists clenched, the cross in his ear swinging back and forth like a pendulum.

Rose began to say, "Just because you can't see or touch something doesn't mean that—

Larry cut her off. "When did you take that picture of Mrs. Lunardi, Madison?"

My mind whirred until I came up with the answer. "A week ago. Sunday."

And then I got it: I'd taken the picture five days before Mrs. Lunardi died. She wasn't a ghost, after all.

Either I was completely insane, or there was another explanation.

"You want to go for a walk?" Duncan asked me outside the purple door. "We can go back to that spot by the rocks and take pictures or . . . whatever."

The thought of "whatever" made me smile. Maybe living in Sandyland wouldn't be so awful. Maybe it would even be . . . okay.

"I'd like that," I said. "But I have to do something with my parents." He didn't have to know about the apartment hunting.

Not yet. I was still getting used to the idea.

"So you and your parents are pretty tight?" he asked.

I snorted. "Hardly. We each kind of do our own thing." I shrugged. "It works out okay." Except for when it doesn't.

"That's cool," he said.

"You and your father seem close."

"I guess." He bit his lip. I really liked that little chip in his tooth. "But we're like buddies, you know? Like, he'll go out on the boat for a couple of days, and it's cool. Or, I'll stay out all night, and he doesn't care. So—I guess I'm lucky. You know, because I can do pretty much whatever I want. Larry's a cool guy. We get along."

"I always wished I had a sister," I said. "Or maybe even a brother. Just—someone besides me."

He glanced at Psychic Photo's front door. "Yeah—me, too. Hangin' with Leo and Delilah, it almost feels like we're related. And . . . it's nice." Something passed over his face—thoughts about leaving Sandyland, maybe?

He took both of my hands in his and looked straight at me, his eyes like sea glass. "Can I see you tonight?"

I moved toward him. "I think that can be arranged."

We held each other's gaze, and he might have kissed me if a married couple in matching red polo shirts hadn't completely ruined the moment by making us move so they could get to the door. (As he looked at the shop's sign, the man remarked, "Do you think we'll have to tell them we want some photos printed or will they just *know?*")

I gave Duncan's hands one last squeeze. "Nine o'clock?"

"Meet you here."

16.

MY PARENTS GOT ALL GUSSIED UP to look at apartments: a button-down shirt for my dad, a flowered summer dress for my mom. They shouldn't have bothered. If Home Suite Home was craptacular, then the apartments we saw were suckerific. I didn't take any pictures. If there were ghosts in these places, they were sure to be mean ones.

Apartment #1 (a.k.a. "The Carbon Monoxide Special") was right down the road from Home Suite Home—if you can call a six-lane highway a road. There was no tiny hill between it and the highway, though, no oxygen-producing grass to filter the fumes.

"It's quieter in the winter," the apartment manager shouted, pulling down a squeaky window, "when it's all closed up."

"Why can't we just rent something near the beach?" I asked as we drove to the next place. That would make it easier to get out for moonlit strolls with Duncan.

"For the same reason we have to live here in the first place," my mother said.

Apartment #2 (code word: "Cave") was in an okay-ish neighborhood of squatty houses and patchy lawns. My mother said the houses on that street cost almost a million dollars because they were on the ocean side of the highway, but I think she was making that up. The neighborhood didn't look beachy at all. It looked like it could be in Amerige, like it could be anywhere.

The Cave was at the end of a cul-de-sac, part of a beat-up blue house that backed up to a hill. The apartment had a side door and a tiny window—and that was it. The rest of it was buried in the slope. Inside it was quiet and cool. Actually, it was kind of cold—and it was over eighty degrees outside. It felt like we were in a tomb.

What would this place be like in January? When my dad (he'd shaved!) asked about fire safety, the homeowner, a grizzled old man who looked about a hundred miserable years old, said there was a door that led to the main house, "But I keep it locked at all times."

Next!

We ended our "Beautiful Homes of Sandyland" tour at a complex called Valley View Apartments. I spent the entire time there trying to pick a more descriptive name. The Pit? The Hole? The Place Where Ugly People Come to Die?

The apartments weren't so much in a valley as they were in an enormous ditch. It made The Cave seem cheery in comparison: at least there you got sunlight in the yard. At Valley View it, would always be night. It was like December in Sweden or Alaska or one of those other northern places where the sun doesn't shine. Swear to God: it was after one o'clock when we saw the place, and the sun hadn't risen over the hill yet.

130

On the plus side, I wouldn't want to see this place brightly lit. Even in darkness it looked dirty, worn down, and just plain sad. There were two long, brown buildings that faced each other over a central parking lot. There were no patios or balconies, just straight concrete walkways, both upstairs and down, with a row of front doors. A couple of the doors had fake-flower wreaths or cutesy welcome signs on them, which made them seem even more pathetic, somehow. The complex was filled with fat adults and skinny children, all walking with their shoulders hunched forward, their mouths turned down. Televisions blared behind every door.

I thought, *I would rather die than live here*.

Following the apartment manager to "a nice corner unit," we smelled something nasty, and then we saw it: a pile of pinkish beige vomit right in the middle of the walkway. The manager walked around it. My mother stopped dead and grabbed my arm, as if pulling me back from a speeding car.

"I'll get someone to clean that up," said the manager, a cigarette-stained woman with yellow hair and gray teeth and a frightening set of boobs that threatened to spill out of a sparkly turquoise tank top.

"We're finished here," my mother said, her voice hoarse. And then she turned and pulled me to the car, my father following.

We climbed into the Escalade, which looked completely out of place in the lot of junk cars. And then my mother burst into tears. She cried and cried till she almost couldn't breathe, her sharp shoulders hunching forward just like the people who lived at Valley View.

She was still crying by the time we pulled into the lot at Home

Suite Home—which, I gotta tell you, was looking like a five-star resort at this point—but she was breathing a little more normally and cleaning herself up with a worn tissue. I should have felt sorry for her, I guess, but all I could think about was the vomit.

After my father parked the car, my mother stayed in her seat. He came around, opened her door, and helped her out.

I didn't even notice Duncan until I practically tripped over him. He was crouched on the concrete outside our door, writing a note. When he saw me, he grabbed the note, along with a bouquet of wildflowers that had been resting on the ground, and scrambled to his feet.

"Hi." His eyes looked especially green in the sunlight. The bleached tips of his hair sprouted from beneath his backward baseball cap.

"Hi," I said. You'd think I'd be worried about what my parents would think of Duncan, but right now I was just mortified to be seen with them, my father supporting my teary-eyed mother's arm like she was out on a day pass from the mental hospital.

"I didn't think you were here," he said, holding up the note.

"I wasn't." I took the slip of paper.

"Oh."

My parents scurried past him with barely a hello. At least my mother wasn't actively crying at this point.

"We were just running some errands," I lied.

He nodded and handed me the bouquet.

"These are for me?" I said. (All together now: "No, duh!") There were wild daisies and Queen Anne's lace and some purple flowers I didn't recognize.

"They grow on the hill behind my apartment," he said. "They

132

looked really pretty, so I just, like, thought of you."

"Thanks." A funny feeling spread through my chest.

"They might have bugs," he said.

"Oh!" I held the flowers farther away from my face and then looked at him. "There's something different about you."

He touched his earlobe. "I took my earrings out. I thought I might be meeting your parents."

My chest tightened further. Anxiety: that's what it was. I wasn't just embarrassed about my mother. I felt really uncomfortable having Duncan so close to my parents, like they were from two different worlds that I'd rather not mix.

"I better see how my mom's doing," I mumbled.

He nodded. "Yeah, I gotta get home anyway."

"Where do you live?"

He gestured to the hills beyond the highway. "About a mile from here there's this group of apartments. It's called Valley View."

My hands clutched the flowers. "I think I've seen it," I croaked.

"Yeah?" He looked pleased. "It's pretty nice. A lot better than the last place we lived."

He reached out to touch my cheek, but when he saw my expression, he stopped. "So—I'll see you tonight?"

I nodded at the flowers, not wanting to meet his eyes. "Nine o'clock."

Inside our room I sat on the couch and opened Duncan's note. It was in all capitals. His handwriting was so weird and spiky, it looked like he had held the pen with his teeth.

DEAR MADSON (GG),
YOU ARE A RELLY NICE GRILL IM GLAD I MET YOU I
CANT WEIGHT FOR TONITE.
DUNCAN

I stared at the note for what felt like an hour. And then I crumpled it up and threw it in the trash.

17.

THERE'S NOTHING LIKE A GOOD FUNERAL to cheer a person up, and by the next afternoon my mother was downright chipper.

"Mrs. Lunardi was sixty-six years old," she chirped, kicking off the sneakers she had worn to work. "Cancer. Had it for years. Went away a few times, but it kept coming back." She pulled off her green polo shirt and stood there in a beige bra while she finished talking. "She lived in Sandyland her whole life—should be a big crowd."

"Sounds awesome," I said, the sarcasm completely lost on her.

She took a new-ish peach T-shirt out of her drawer and pulled it over her head. "Two big arrangements around the casket—I did white roses and calla lilies—plus three on the altar. And those were just from the family. We had *eighteen* orders from people around town. Hydrangeas, lilies—no carnations allowed on my watch." She plucked a comb from the dresser and began to smooth her yellow hair. "The floral manager said she'd never seen anyone work as fast as me. She said I was a natural."

"I'm really happy for you, Mom. If you're lucky, maybe some other people around here will die."

Whoops—there was that eyebrow crease.

"I'm just doing this for my family," she said.

I nodded, feeling ashamed at my jerkiness. But I didn't want to hear about Francine Lunardi or Sandyland or carnations. I didn't care whether the guy in the window was a mysterious spirit or a garden-variety perv. I just wanted to go home to Amerige, where life was normal. Where *people* were normal.

I hadn't gone to meet Duncan the night before. And I knew that was jerky of me (are we sensing a pattern here?), but I couldn't get beyond the way I felt when I'd seen him near my parents. I couldn't move beyond my reaction to his note. I couldn't stop thinking, *He's just like Kyle Ziegenfuss, only cuter.*

If Duncan showed up in Amerige, I wouldn't look at him twice. What was I doing, spending time with him here? Sure, I looked like a freak myself, with the awful clothes and the worse hair, but I was still *me*. Deep down, I was still one of the good kids. I could fix my hair and buy new clothes, and I'd be right back to the person I'd always been.

I wasn't sure how I felt about Delilah, either. She was fun for a summer friend, like a temporary, off-the-wall fill-in for Lexie, but I couldn't see us being best buds if I was actually going to live here.

Was I really going to live here? Oh, God. How did this happen?

I kept picturing my house like a photograph in my mind. Our five-bedroom model on Jennifer Road was called "The Tuscany." It was stucco and stack stone with high ceilings and wrought iron railings. We'd moved there four years ago, from a smaller, older house across town.

Right away my mother had gotten rid of our old furniture and bought stuff that matched the house: heavy and ornate, with velvet upholstery and touches of gold. Then a couple of years later we went to France for spring break, and my mother ditched it all for "French Country," which meant distressed wood and checked prints and roosters. Lots and lots of roosters.

Maybe if she had saved that money instead of spending it all on roosters, we'd still have the house. But no. It was more than that: it was the pool, the cars, the televisions. It was the vacations and the dinners out. It was everything that made up our lives.

And now it was gone.

When my father got home from work, around dinnertime, he was looking considerably less chipper than my mother. If he'd looked tired after his first day of work, today he looked devastated. Without being asked, I got him a glass of ice water. He nodded his thanks and downed it in one gulp.

"Talked to my boss," he said. "He's okay with me taking Wednesday off—Thursday, too, if I need it."

"To go to Amerige?" I asked.

He nodded.

Lexie was back from the lake. What I wouldn't give to talk to her right now. Maybe she could think of some way to convince my parents to stay in town.

"I'm going with you," I announced.

"It's going to be a really short trip," my father said.

"I know."

And then, in a flash, I remembered something Delilah had said about Duncan—that if his father left, he could move in with them.

Of course! I could live with Lexie! Why hadn't I thought of it sooner? Her family loved me, her house was huge, and I was over there all the time, anyway.

"You sure you want to go back?" my mother said. "It's going to be kind of . . . awkward. And, anyway, I have to stay here; I'm scheduled to work Wednesday."

"I'm going."

Tuesday morning, I ran into Delilah on the beach, down where I'd photographed Francine Lunardi. I'd snapped probably fifty shots without enjoying any of them—and without a single inexplicable figure showing up. It was starting to feel like I'd dreamed the whole thing.

"Hey, stranger," Delilah said.

"What do you mean? I saw you, like, three days ago."

"Just giving you a hard time." She smiled, but her eyes looked icier than before. "You want to hang out at the shop with me? I started my landfill piece."

I got the feeling that she was testing me—like she already knew what I was going to say. "Thanks, but I've got to do some things back at the motel."

"Duncan is at the shop," Delilah said. "Just, you know—hanging."

I thought of Duncan's note. *YOU ARE A RELLY NICE GRILL.* If it had happened to somebody else, it would have been funny.

"He missed you the other night," Delilah said.

138

"Oh—right. I just got—my parents had some things they wanted me to do, and they wouldn't let me go." Lame. Very lame.

Delilah nodded, clearly not believing me at all. "He likes you," she said.

"Yeah, I got that." Sweat from my hand dampened my camera.

"And do you . . . feel the same?"

I chose my words carefully. "He's a nice guy."

"Oh." Something in her face shut down. What did it matter, though, what Delilah thought about me? And what difference would it make if I liked Duncan?

"I'm leaving tomorrow," I said. "Going home."

She looked surprised. "Forever?"

I shrugged. "Probably."

Of course, I couldn't be sure that Lexie's parents would let me live with them. But even if I came back to Sandyland, I needed a new crowd—that much was obvious.

She crossed her arms. "That's too bad. We all thought you might—whatever." She studied me with her clear eyes. "It's been fun," she said finally.

"Right," I said. "It has."

18.

THE SUN WAS HIGH IN THE SKY by the time we drove into Amerige. I asked my dad to take me to Lexie's right away because I couldn't stand to go another minute without talking to her. Also, I wasn't quite ready to see my house with a sign out front.

The Larstroms' house was white stucco with a red-tile roof and all kinds of arches and curves that cast interesting shadows. It seemed to have gotten bigger in the time I'd been gone. Had it been only a week and a half? I felt like a completely different person. I needed Lexie to make me feel like myself again.

My dad waited in the car while I went up to the house.

"Goodness, Madison—your hair!" Mrs. Larstrom said, standing in the towering doorway. "I almost didn't recognize you."

"Yeah, it's, um—it was kind of a mistake. Is Lexie here?"

"You just missed Alexis; she's at Melissa's." She touched my arm lightly, her forehead crinkled in concern. "You know Melissa? From the newspaper?"

"Sure, I know Melissa," I told Mrs. Larstrom. My body felt all hot-and-cold. Outside, the air hung heavy and still, while beyond the doorway, the Larstroms' air-conditioning blew full force.

"There were a few kids going over there to swim," Mrs. Larstrom said, touching my arm again. "I'm sure they'd love to see you. Come on in—I'll write down the address."

I mouthed "one minute" to my father and followed Mrs. Larstrom inside. Her footsteps echoed on the marble flooring as I waited in the foyer, the two-story ceiling towering above me, the air-conditioning chilling my veneer of sweat.

It took her a while to come back because the house was so huge. (She'd hardly even notice if I moved in.)

"Here it is," she said, clicking across the marble, holding out a slip of paper, and touching my shoulder. I don't think she'd touched me this much in all the years I'd known her.

She tilted her head to one side. "How are you doing?"

I shrugged. "Okay."

"And your parents?"

"They're good. My dad's in the car."

She nodded. "And your mom?"

"She's at the summer house." It just slipped out. *The summer house*: like we were on a splashy vacation—like we could afford one house, much less two. "She loves the beach," I added.

"Well, Madison, I hope you know that you're always welcome to stay with us. A weekend, a week—as long as you want to visit."

I smiled, quivering with relief. "Thanks. I'll remember that."

Melissa's house, less than a mile away, was almost as big as Lexie's but not nearly as pretty. It was tall and boxy, the brick around the front door too new and too red. The pool was just a normal

141

concrete pool, no boulders or anything, but there was an above-ground hot tub under a thatched roof, like a tiki hut.

The hot tub was so crammed with bodies that I didn't see Lexie at first. Already I was feeling shy and like maybe I shouldn't have told my father to leave.

"Madeleine, was it?" Melissa's mother, Mrs. Raffman, asked me. She was wearing shorts and a tank top that exposed tanned, squishy arms.

"Madison."

"Right." Like Melissa, she had dark, curly hair—though hers was cut short—brown eyes and olive skin. Her mouth smiled but her eyes didn't. She didn't look mean or anything, just tired.

"Melissa, you have another friend here," she called across the yard. Squeals and laughter spilled from the hot tub.

Melissa, in a yellow bikini, appeared from under the tiki hut. She grabbed a towel and padded over the concrete, squinting in the sunlight.

She stopped short when she saw me. *Madison?* She held her hand over her eyes to block the sun but continued to squint; normally she wore heavy black eyeglasses.

"Hey," I said. Her mother slipped back into the house.

"I thought," Melissa began. "I heard . . ."

Across the yard, shady faces peered from under the thatched roof. The squealing stopped.

Melissa said, "You changed your hair."

I touched my head. My black locks were pulled back in a ponytail to minimize the effect. "Yeah, thought I'd try something different. Anyway, I just thought I'd stop by," I said. "Hope it's okay."

"Of *course* it's okay!" Melissa took my arm and pulled me across the concrete. "It's so great to *see* you!"

Celia's face was the first one I recognized. "I thought you moved," she blurted. She was sitting on the edge of the tub, bent over to avoid hitting the roof. She gave me a quick once-over. Suddenly, I wished I had gone to my own house before coming here, if only so I could have changed into something other than the purple shirt and cutoff shorts.

"Madison!" Lexie splashed out of the tub and clamored across the concrete. She was wearing a bright blue bikini top with brown board shorts. My own new bathing suit was in my beach bag. I'd thought about changing before coming over here, but that seemed too pushy, like I was inviting myself to Melissa's pool party instead of just casually stopping by.

Lexie barely even looked at me, just wrapped her skinny arms around me and held me tight—which would have been sweet if she weren't soaking wet or if I'd been in a swimsuit. She said, "Oh, my God! Oh, my God!" in a voice that sounded slightly hysterical. I'd been missing her like crazy, but right now she was kind of embarrassing me.

When she finally let go, there was a wet stain all up my front. I crossed my arms, but it didn't do much good.

"I went to your house; your mom said you were here," I told Lexie, as if this were just a normal summer day. I looked at Melissa. "I hope it's okay," I said for the second time.

"I'm glad you're here," Melissa said. "This was just a last-minute thing, you know—to give the new staff an opportunity to get to know each other better."

I looked at the hot tub and forced a smile at the faces peering back at me. I knew some people. Rolf was there, submerged up to his chest, his bright white arms spread-eagled around the edge of the tub. He wasn't anywhere near Celia. His blue eyes cut into me, a tentative smile on his lips. I flushed with shame—at my hair, at my clothes, at Lexie's outburst.

I had a sudden urge to pull Lexie aside and ask her what else Rolf had said about me since her last e-mail. I'd been so pissed off during the whole Celia thing, but now, looking at him—a smart, cute, normal guy—getting back together seemed less like an opportunity for revenge and more like a chance for forgiveness. We all make mistakes, after all.

"How long are you here?" Lexie asked. "Does this mean you're not moving?"

"It's kind of open-ended," I said, remembering Mrs. Larstrom's words: *as long as you want to stay.*

"I wish you'd told me you were coming," Lexie said.

"It was kind of last-minute." Wasn't she happy to see me? And then I realized: she wouldn't have bothered with this pool party thing if she'd known she could spend the day with me.

"You want something to drink?" Melissa asked. "We've got bottled cappuccinos, plus there's some smoothie left in the blender."

"Um, no thanks."

Celia hauled herself out of the hot tub and clomped across the concrete on her big duck feet. I still couldn't believe that Rolf had dumped me for her. She wasn't even pretty. The water had slicked her hair back from her face. Her forehead looked very high and eggheady.

"So, what does this mean?" Celia said, hands on hips.

I squinted at her, confused. "Um, I'm not that thirsty."

"No," she snapped. "What does it mean that you're back? Melissa?"

Melissa cleared her throat and looked at the ground. Drops of chlorinated water dripped off her curls. "Wow. This is awkward."

"What?" I asked.

"Everyone said you'd moved." She looked at me before dropping her eyes back to the ground. "And then Celia called a couple of days ago and asked if we still needed a photographer for the paper. She'd been the runner-up, and so I just, um . . ."

"But I told you I was staying!" I said. "In that e-mail!"

"I know, but my parents know some people who know your parents. And they said—and obviously it was just a rumor—that your dad's business went bankrupt and you lost everything and that there was no way you could afford to stay in town. And so I sent you another e-mail, just to make sure you were coming back, but you didn't answer it, and your cell phone had been cut off, and . . ." She looked up, desperate. "Are you sure you don't want a cappuccino?"

I nodded.

"Did you bring your suit?" Melissa asked, changing the subject. "Do you want to come in the hot tub? The pool's pretty cold."

I did a yes-no, nod-shake: I'd brought my suit, but I didn't want to go in the tub. "Thanks, but I've got some things to do at my house." Could I even call it "my house" anymore?

"Oh," Melissa said. "Sure." Celia retreated to the hot tub, claiming a spot far from Rolf.

"Can I use your phone?" I asked Melissa, suddenly desperate to flee. I was about to say that I'd forgotten my cell, but then I remembered: they all knew I no longer had one.

"Why don't you walk home with me?" Lexie said, touching my arm just as her mother had done. "You can call from there."

I nodded, too afraid I'd cry if I tried to say anything.

"We can work something out," Melissa said. "Like, maybe Celia takes the sports photos and you take the candids. Or something."

I nodded again.

My camera was in my bag, but I didn't take it out. There was nothing about this moment that I wanted to preserve.

Lexie's house wasn't far. Our flip-flops sounded like fat raindrops slapping against the tree-shaded pavement.

"I thought you were gone," Lexie said in a quiet voice. "I mean, like, forever." Now that her blond hair had begun to dry in the late-morning heat, I could see that she'd gotten it cut—straight and blunt, just below her shoulders. We were no longer twins.

"Why would you think that?" I asked, annoyed. I'd been away for less than two weeks. Some people left town for the entire summer, and it was no big deal.

"Because your house has a big sign out front, and you never even told me you were moving." She glanced at me and then quickly looked away. "I tried calling, but your phone's been disconnected."

"I'll get a new cell," I said. "Eventually." And I would, too. Cell phones weren't that expensive. Everyone I knew had one—okay, everyone except Leo and Delilah and Duncan. But they didn't count.

"No, I mean your real phone—your home phone. I called it

and got this recording. 'The number you are trying to reach has been disconnected.' And I got a couple of e-mails from you and then—nothing." Why did she have that tone in her voice? It sounded like she was accusing me of something.

"You make it sound like I died," I said.

"You should have told me you were moving," she said.

"I didn't know!" I stopped in front of a pretty blue house with a flowering tree out front. There was a gardener truck parked by the curb, a quiet man in a straw hat snipping at the hedges. A few years earlier my father had built an addition on the back of this house, enlarging the kitchen and creating a big family room with skylights. The kitchen had a brick pizza oven and a special freezer just for ice cream. My father talked about that freezer for months.

Lexie faced me. She looked sad or—something. I couldn't quite figure it out.

"My dad got some work at the beach," I explained. "And they made it seem like it was just a vacation for my mom and me to come with—you know, to make up for the cruise. But then we got there and they started acting all weird, and they finally admitted that they'd lost the house, and—" My voice cracked. I swallowed hard to keep from crying.

"I know," Lexie said. "My mom told me about your dad's business."

"Your mom knows?"

"Everyone does."

"Great." I shut my eyes for a minute. When I opened them, I was still standing in front of a house I'd passed a hundred times, looking at the friend who'd seen me through a million problems.

147

But it was like I'd been dropped into an alternate universe. Neither the house nor Lexie seemed entirely real.

"We're poor," I said. "My dad's digging holes for a living. My mom got a job at a grocery store. It's like a bad dream." I regretted the words the instant I spoke them: saying them out loud made the whole thing real.

We were quiet for the rest of the walk. By the time we got to Lexie's, sweat was slithering down my neck and back. The air-conditioning in her house gave me the shakes. Her mother made a brief appearance—just long enough to tap my arm and squeeze my hand—and then we went up to Lexie's room. The upstairs hallway was quiet; the housekeeper was off today, and Brooke and Kenzie were at gymnastics camp.

I sprawled out on Lexie's fluffy bed, but she perched far away from me, on the swivel chair by her computer. "Is it nice there?" she asked. "At the beach?"

"It sucks," I said to her ceiling.

"I'm sorry."

"It's okay," I said. "I'm not staying."

"Where are you going?"

I sat up on the bed and looked around. Lexie's room was almost as big as the suite in Sandyland: plenty of room for two people. Of course, Lexie had never had to share a room; maybe she wouldn't like it. There was a tiny guest room down the hall. I didn't need a lot of space.

"I was thinking," I began. "Your mom said . . ." My voice trailed off. Lexie stayed frozen in her chair. This visit wasn't going quite the way I'd expected it to. That whole stop at Melissa's had really thrown things off.

I grabbed a throw pillow and flopped back down on the bed. "I hate Celia," I blurted, back in familiar territory.

"What? Oh, yeah. She's such a bitch."

"Did you see the way she was looking at me? And how she came running out of the hot tub?"

Lexie's face relaxed. "She's like a vulture. Seriously. I can't believe she'd just call Melissa up like that. . . ."

I rolled over onto one side and propped my head on an elbow. "She won't let me have anything to myself. Photography. Rolf. I don't even think she liked Rolf until I went out with him."

"You never really went out with him," Lexie said, turning to the computer and poking a couple of keys.

I sat up. "Well, I sort of did. You know what I mean."

"Celia's a bitch," she said, turning back to me, holding fast to the chair. "And I don't even think she's that good a photographer."

"So what did Rolf say about me?" I asked. "Weren't you going to talk to him?"

She popped up from her chair and headed for her bathroom. "I gotta get out of this suit. It's totally clammy."

While she showered and changed, I sat on her bed, hugging my knees to my chest, trying to find the right words. When the bathroom door finally opened, I just blurted it out.

"I was thinking I could come live with you."

She didn't say anything for the longest time, just stared at me with those blue Larstrom eyes. "I don't think your parents would let you," she said finally.

"I think they would." I spoke fast. "I've been thinking about it a lot, and I know they feel really bad about moving me like this, right in the middle of high school. Besides, I don't think Sandyland's got a very good school system. My parents are always saying they want me to go to a good college, and now I'll need a scholarship, which means my record matters even more. It's not like I wouldn't see them. They're only a couple of hours away, and there's a train."

"Maddy, you're my best friend, and I love you," Lexie said, her voice cracking.

"I love you, too, Lex!" Relief surged through my chest. Everything was going to be okay. So why did she look so miserable?

"But there's no way," she began. "I mean, my parents can't just take in another kid—"

"But your mom said it was okay!" I said. "Not to live here, exactly, but she said I could stay as long as I wanted. And I can help out—you know, do chores and stuff. And I could babysit Brooke and Kenzie. And maybe my parents could pay some kind of rent."

There was a knock on the door, and Mrs. Larstrom stuck her head in. "There's a visitor downstairs," she told us.

The visitor was Rolf. I saw the top of his head as soon as I reached the staircase. As I headed downstairs, my brain was a jumble: *Rolf likes me. But Lexie doesn't want me living here. So it doesn't matter if Rolf wants to get back together. Nothing matters if I'm stuck in Sandyland. Life here will go on without me.*

Mrs. Larstrom was standing at the bottom of the enormous winding stairway, a strained smile on her face. Mrs. Larstrom would let me live here. She'd said I could stay as long as I wanted. Brooke and Kenzie would love to have me around; I was always a lot nicer to them than Lexie was. And as for Lexie: I shouldn't have sprung it on her like that. She'd come around once she got used to the idea.

For the moment, I would concentrate on Rolf. He was right there, standing just inside the towering front doorway, looking cute and smart and, well, *normal* in a white surf T-shirt and board shorts, a JanSport backpack slung over one shoulder.

My hand firmly on the staircase's polished rail, I smiled at him—or I tried to, at any rate. He scrunched up his baby face with an emotion that looked something like anticipation but more like—what? Confusion? Fear? Embarrassment?

And then his eyes flicked beyond me, above me, and his face softened. You might even say he began to glow, if that's not too girly a word. No, it wasn't too girly at all; it was perfectly girly. He glowed, the soft little pansy. Totally glowed—but not for me.

I halted and spun around. Lexie stood a few steps above me, her head hanging low. And that's when I got it.

No wonder Lexie didn't want me living here. She was much too busy with Rolf.

"I didn't think I'd see you for a while," my dad said when I walked in the back door of our house (Lexie's mom drove me). He was in the kitchen wrapping things in newspaper and putting them into cardboard boxes. His movements were stiff, slow, his heavy body defeated by a day of ditchdigging followed by an afternoon of packing. "I figured you'd spend the night at Lexie's."

I shook my head. He didn't ask me to explain, which I appreciated.

There was more to pack than I'd have expected, when you considered that most of our furniture had been repossessed. I put my clothes in a suitcase, my yearbooks and photo albums into cardboard boxes. My Mac had to be returned, but I backed up my files onto a zip drive before my dad put the computer into its original packaging (my mom was a big box saver) and drove it back to the store with a few words of wisdom: "Don't ever buy something on credit."

"Thanks, Dad. I'll try to remember that."

I didn't dare complain. While I'd been having my heart stomped on at Lexie's house, my dad had been trading in his beloved Escalade for a faded tan minivan of uncertain vintage. My mom's BMW was absent from its spot in the garage. I didn't ask any questions.

By ten thirty at night, it was done: every detail of our entire lives had been packed away or tossed. There had been papers signed, phone calls made. There was nothing left to do, nothing left to hope for.

"I saved out some blankets and pillows," my dad said, crumpling a sauce-stained Taco Bell wrapper from dinner. "We can sleep on the library floor—that carpet's pretty padded. I've got nothing left to do here, so we can leave first thing in the morning. Unless you want to spend a little more time with your friends, say your good-byes . . ."

I gazed at the empty room, the sad picture hooks on the butter-colored walls. "Let's get out of here."

"Now?"

"Now."

We shoved four suitcases, two laundry baskets, a cardboard box, and a whole bunch of overflowing shopping bags into the beige van. The rest of our stuff, safely stored in a cinder-block storage unit, could wait. We probably didn't even need all of these clothes and papers and books, which would just make the suite seem smaller.

Once the house was empty, I thought about going from room to room and taking photographs. But I didn't. It wasn't just because the day was so sad, the house no longer ours. It's because sometimes things are best remembered in your heart.

"Did you have a nice time with your friends?" my dad asked as we pulled out of the driveway for the final time, the FOR SALE: BANK-OWNED PROPERTY sign illuminated by the landscape lighting, the raggedy yard looking better in the semidarkness.

"Sure," I said. "A great time."

On the way out of our development, we passed two other Tuscany models, plus three Santa Fes and one English Cottage. I said good-bye to Jennifer Road and my favorite street in the development, Noah Way, which sounds just like "no way" if you say it fast enough. On Amerige Road we passed my favorite Starbucks, my elementary school, the movie theater. We zipped right by the turnoff to our first house, the little house, the one that wasn't good enough.

Finally we got on the highway, and the van picked up speed.

"Well, that's done," my dad said.

"Yes," I agreed. "It is."

19.

It was almost one o'clock in the afternoon by the time I woke up on my scratchy couch at Home Suite Home. I'd finally mastered the art of sleeping through the cacophony of gurgling pipes, barking dogs, and sleeping children. I was alone in the room; my parents were both at work.

It was a beautiful day: blue sky, light breeze, low humidity. I kept the curtains shut, preferring to bask in darkness and depression. Now that the shock of Lexie's betrayal had sunk in ("We didn't mean for it to happen," she'd said. And—make me spew— "It's like we're two halves of a whole." Come! On! Who says crap like that?) I realized how much I'd been counting on her to save me. I'd built up this whole fantasy of "Life with the Larstroms." In that world, nothing much would change. I'd have the same school and the same friends. Lexie would take me shopping and put everything on her credit card; her mother would never notice. I'd miss my parents—I mean, sort of—but it's not like I'd never see them again.

But like I said, that had been a fantasy. My old life was over. This was the reality: instead of being a princess in the Larstroms' palace, I was a prisoner in a cut-rate motel. In place of Lexie and her funny e-mails, I had Delilah and her garbage collection. Instead of Rolf and his fizzy juices, I had Duncan and his beat-up skateboard.

At the thought of Duncan, my eyes filled with tears. Why was he laughing all the time? Didn't he know that his life sucked?

In the dingy room, I sorted through my clothes from home, most of which were even more worn-out than I'd remembered. My purple thrift-shop shirt looked new in comparison. At least my Seven jeans still looked good. I pulled them on, thinking they'd make me feel like myself again. They didn't, but I kept them on anyway. I went outside to the little patio, sat on a dirty plastic chair, and listened to the passing cars.

Hours later, my mother, getting ready for bed, said, "Someone stopped by to see you yesterday."

Duncan. Had he remembered to take out his earrings? Had he left me another embarrassing note?

"It was a girl," my mother said. "With sort of . . . strange hair. And clothes."

I felt relieved and disappointed all at once. "That's Delilah. She's an artist."

"Apparently." My mother squirted some white lotion onto her hands. "She wanted you to stop by."

I shrugged. "I'll go tomorrow." (Maybe.)

"She said something about . . . a man in a window?" She rubbed the lotion into her hands. "She said you'd know what she meant."

I stared at my mother. "What about him?"

My mother snapped the top on her bottle. "She said she knows who he is."

I heard the music long before I reached Psychic Photo—or, rather, I felt the beats pounding the night air. It wasn't until I was right outside the building that I managed to decipher the lyrics: something about a love roller coaster. Tell me about it.

The back door was unlocked, the door at the bottom of the stairs propped open. I thought of the strange man sneaking around. They should really be more careful.

Music wasn't the only thing coming out of the apartment. People stood jammed along the stairs and in the doorway: major fire hazard. I pushed my way past the warm, sticky bodies. Someone spilled a plastic cup of soda on me. It skimmed my tank top and soaked into my expensive jeans.

I fought my way into the crammed apartment, my senses instantly overloaded by throbbing disco music, laughter, dancing bodies, and diamonds of light from the mirrored ball. The room smelled of sweat and scented shampoo, cookies and chips and salsa.

Where was Delilah? Or Duncan? Was there anyone here I knew? Finally, I spotted Leo. I don't know how I missed him jumping around in the middle of the dance floor (otherwise known as a small patch of rug where the couch once sat), posing every now and then with one hand in the air. He wore a white suit, too loose and too short, and a dark shirt: deep purple or maybe navy.

Dancing with him was a heavy girl dressed in a low-cut red tank top, a tight black miniskirt, and ripped fishnet stockings.

Her black hair was cut in a severe bob, the bangs ending in a straight line a good inch above her penciled-in eyebrows. Her eyeliner and lipstick were black. Her ears, nose, and lip were all pierced. Other parts of her were probably pierced as well, but I didn't want to think about it.

Most of the kids in the room looked more average—jeans, shorts, T-shirts—but they all seemed a little, I don't know, shabby. Their clothes were worn, their haircuts ratty. And I fit right in.

I pushed closer to the dance floor, checking faces. Duncan would be out here. He was the kind of person who liked to be in the middle of things, to laugh and dance and live in the moment. And why not? In his world, odds were good that tomorrow would be worse than today.

But he wasn't there. Leo caught my eye and waved. I waved back before turning around to search for Delilah.

That's when I saw Duncan. He was all alone, slumped on the couch, which had been pushed against the wall in front of the window. The window was wide open—no wonder you could hear the music from the street—but there was no one lurking on the other side, at least that I could see. Duncan was not laughing, dancing, or seizing the moment. In fact, he looked completely miserable, just staring into space, his arms crossed in front of his chest.

So he was not all sunshine and light, after all. Duncan had a crappy life, and he knew it. We were more alike than I had realized.

I worked my way toward him, suddenly desperate to make him smile. When I reached the side of the couch, I bent down and whispered in his ear, "Arnold? Egbert? Burl?"

He looked up and his mouth dropped open. "You."

"Francis?" I said. "Horace?" When he didn't say anything, just continued to stare, I said, "Your real name must be totally dweeby. Otherwise, you'd just tell me what it is."

A smile spread across his face. But it wasn't his usual life's-a-party grin; it was more like . . . wonder. And joy. Like: tonight was a birthday party and Christmas morning and a trip to Disney World all in one.

I settled on the arm of the couch. "Unless you have a girl's name," I continued. "I've heard of guys named, like, Carroll. And Marion. And this guy I knew in junior high? He was named *Ashley*. I'm serious. Total psycho—he beat the crap out of anyone who even looked at him funny."

Duncan began to laugh: that crazy, infectious sound. I thought, *Dang, I'm funny*, and prepared to launch into another monologue. But he stopped me.

"I thought you'd gone." He took my hand. I never knew that someone's hand could feel so good.

I looked at my feet. "I'm sorry I didn't show up the other night. Something came up, and I didn't have your phone number, and then I had to go out of town. . . ."

"So you're staying?"

"It looks that way." What was that stupid thing people said? *This is the first day of the rest of your life*. "Yeah, I'm staying."

For now, that was all I wanted to say on the subject. "My mom said Delilah stopped by, that she knew who the guy in the photo was." Behind us, a cool breeze slipped through the window.

"Oh, yeah. I'll let her tell you about it. She's probably hiding in her room. She hates Leo's parties." We got off the couch and he guided me through the crowd by my hand.

When we got to the bedroom doorway, he turned around and gazed into my eyes, his expression so intense, so adoring, that I had to look away. "I missed you," he said. "I was just totally—I just totally missed you."

The bottom of my stomach fell to the floor. Duncan hadn't been upset because his life was so crappy. It was all about me. Wow. Go figure.

Since her half of the room was next to the bathroom, Delilah had retreated to the far side of the curtain. She sat on Leo's orange bed, huge noise-blocking headphones hugging her ears, bent over a sketch pad. It wasn't as loud as in the living room, but the walls still throbbed.

Something was different about her. And then I realized: the stripes in her hair were now blue instead of pink, all the better to match her blue sundress with white polka dots. She was perfectly dressed for a summer party—in 1958.

Duncan flicked his hand in front of her face to get her attention.

"Madison." She didn't look surprised to see me. She sat up straighter and crossed her arms. "Nice jeans. Seven's, right?"

"Yeah." I touched the soft denim.

"You could get a lot of money for them."

I took a step back as if she might try to take them. There was no way I was giving up my jeans. Delilah just didn't get it.

"My mother said you knew something about the man in the window."

She uncrossed her arms and leaned forward. "He got hit by a car!"

"Yeah, right." I wasn't going to fall for another one of her lines.

"No, really," Duncan said. "He did."

I looked at him and then back at Delilah. "Okay, you're starting to freak me out."

"Tell me about it." She scooted off the bed and went around the curtain to her side of the room. A moment later she was back with the local newspaper.

My legs got so shaky when I saw the man's familiar face on the front page that I had to sit on the bed.

VISITOR STRUCK BY PICKUP TRUCK

By Barbara Harrington for the Sandyland Tribune

Ronald Young, a 34-year-old mechanical engineer from Ottawa, Canada, was seriously injured Tuesday morning when he stepped off the curb on Main Street into the path of an oncoming pickup truck. According to Loretta Pismo, proprietor of I Scream! You Scream! Frozen Treats, Mr. Young bought a raspberry sorbet right before the accident. "He was talking on his cell phone, so I guess he didn't hear the truck coming."

The driver of the truck has been identified as Brett McCordle, age 19, of Sandyland. No charges have been filed at this time.

After witnessing the accident, Ms. Pismo dialed 911. Soon after, an unconscious Mr. Young was rushed by ambulance to the Sandyland Health and Emergency Clinic on Upper Pass Parkway, where he was treated for his immediate injuries by the physician on call, Dr. Lydia Martin. Mr. Young was later airlifted to Green Valley Medical Center.

Mr. Young suffered a broken leg, two broken ribs, a punctured lung, and a concussion. He remains in a coma. It will be several days before doctors can determine whether he has suffered any permanent brain damage.

Mr. Young had been staying at the Beachcomber Inn with his wife, Jennifer Young, aged 30, who revealed that their vacation had begun on a happy note. "A few days ago, we discovered that I am pregnant with our first child. We thought we were entering a whole new chapter of our lives."

When I finished reading, I checked the date of the article. "This is today's paper."

"It happened yesterday," Delilah said.

"So he was fine when I took the photograph—which means he *was* outside your window."

I handed the paper back to Delilah.

Ronald Young was just a creepy Canadian tourist. And Francine Lunardi was just a sick old lady. There were no spirits in the world. There was no magic. There was a rational explanation for everything. And the only rational explanation was this: my mind had been playing tricks.

"When I take pictures, it's like I go into a kind of trance," I said. "I focus on one little thing, whatever I'm going to shoot, and it's like everything else disappears. I didn't think it was possible that a person could be there and I wouldn't see him, but that must be what happened."

"Doesn't he look familiar, though?" she pressed, passing back the paper. "It's driving me crazy that I can't place him."

I studied the grainy black-and-white photo, a casual shot taken on the beach. Ronald Young wore a plain T-shirt and flowered swim trunks.

It hit us at the same time. "The crop and zoom guy!" When I'd seen Ronald Young in the shop, I thought he looked kind. But perverts came in all sorts of packages. Maybe the clueless thing was just an act, an excuse to hang out longer.

"Mystery solved," Delilah said.

Suddenly, I felt very tired and empty.

"So you're going to live with your mom, then?" Delilah asked carefully.

"Well . . . yeah. It looks that way." How did she know I'd been planning to move in with Lexie? Sometimes it really did seem like Delilah had ESP.

"And—is your dad okay with that?"

"Okay with what?"

Duncan put his arm around me. "We thought you were going back to live with your dad."

Okay, now I was confused. "But my dad's here."

"So your parents are getting back together?" Delilah asked.

Then I got it. "You thought my parents were splitting up?" Of course, the thought had crossed my mind, too.

Delilah looked at Duncan and then back at me. "Isn't that why you're here? I mean, you're obviously not on vacation."

"But you saw my parents together," I told Duncan.

He bit his lip, and I remembered that afternoon when we came back from looking at apartments: my mother crying, my father slumped and hopeless. I blushed.

"We lost our house," I said, hating the words. Words made it all real. "And the furniture, the appliances, my computer. And— everything." I swallowed hard. "We lost everything."

"Wow," Duncan said. "That blows."

"Yeah, really. So I'm stuck out here in the middle of *nowhere*, and they act like it's nothing that I had to leave all of my friends."

I caught myself and added, "I mean, most of my friends." What I really wanted to say was "my real friends," but that would have been rude.

"I don't mean to say Sandyland is the middle of nowhere," I added (even though it was). "But I've lived in Amerige my whole life. Plus, I was going to be taking all honors classes this year. My school is, like, one of the best in the state. And I was in peer leadership and choir, and I was even going to work on the newspaper, which was going to look really good on my college applications." I swallowed hard and stopped talking. If I said any more, I'd cry.

"That's great that your parents are back together," Duncan said finally.

"They were never apart," I reminded him.

"It isn't so bad here," Delilah said. "And there's a newspaper at Sandyland High."

"Any good?" I asked, trying to work up some enthusiasm.

She paused, trying to find the perfect words. "It's embarrassingly amateurish," she admitted. "And no one reads it."

"But it would be better if you worked on it," Duncan said, squeezing my hand.

My eyes filled with tears. Duncan was so sweet. Why wasn't that enough?

Someone pushed open the curtain that hung between the two "bedrooms." It was the girl Leo had been dancing with, with the severe black hair and all the piercings.

She pointed her thumb toward the closed bathroom door. "Do you know who'th in there?" she lisped. Apparently, her tongue was pierced, too. Of course it was. "Becauth I've been waiting for, like, ever, and I've really got to take a pith."

At that, the bathroom door opened, and she scurried inside. This was so different from the parties back home.

"I know moving's rough," Duncan said, squeezing my hand. "But I really think you're going to like it here, G.G."

The nickname, which I'd once found funny, suddenly depressed me even more. *I don't even get to keep my own name.*

Duncan insisted on walking me home. But first he insisted on dancing with me. The boy could move, I'll give him that much. It was as if he absorbed the lights and music swirling around us, like they became a part of him.

I wasn't the only one who noticed. Ricki, that girl from the beach, wasn't there, but I caught the pierced "pith" girl shooting him glances, plus this tall girl with super-short brown hair and bright blue eyeglasses kept trying to cut in on me. Duncan just smiled at her and put his hands on my waist.

What would my real friends think if they could see me now? Would they even recognize me? Did I recognize myself?

164

Duncan slipped his hands around my back. I looped mine around his neck and looked into his bright green eyes. It was getting really hot in here.

We touched damp foreheads, his face so close that it looked like he had only one eye. He pulled me toward him and tilted his head to one side for nose clearance. His breath warmed my face.

I jerked my head to one side just before he reached my lips.

"Tell me your name," I commanded into his ear. I needed to know who he was. Without a name, he wasn't quite real.

He stopped dancing. He took a step back. He shook his head once.

And then he walked me home.

"Where was Rose tonight?" I asked as we turned off Main Street. My ears were still rushing from the aftereffect of the music, like I was holding conch shells to my ears. My hand itched with the desire to be held, but Duncan kept his hands in his pockets.

He shrugged. "My house, probably."

"So things are going good with your dad?"

He shook his head. "She just keeps stringing him along." His shoulders pointed slightly forward, as if he were drawing into himself. The streetlights lit his profile. There was a slight bump in the end of his small nose. It suited him somehow, gave him even more character.

We passed the Sandyland Library and the Sandyland Town Hall. The quaint town gave way to dingy mini-marts and auto repair shops. A single car passed. Otherwise, we were alone.

"Will you be a sophomore this year?" I asked when the silence became unbearable. "Or a junior?"

"Sophomore," he said. "They were gonna make me repeat freshman year, but then they figured it was best to just move me along or they'd never get rid of me."

I forced a hollow laugh. "I'll be a sophomore, too. Maybe we'll be in some classes together."

He looked at me, eyebrows raised, and shook his head. "If you were going to be in honors classes at your old school, you know, the *really good one*, you'll be in honors classes here. You'll see a lot of Delilah—she's really smart. I'm in all the dumb classes."

"Don't say that!" I said. *Just like Kyle Ziegenfuss, only cuter.*

He shrugged. "That's what they are. Whatever. I don't show up much, anyway."

My flip-flops seemed loud in the night silence. I chose my words carefully. "A learning disability is nothing to be ashamed of."

"Huh?" He squinted with confusion.

"I've had training," I said. "In my peer leadership program. We went on this retreat last year, and they taught us some techniques. Like, there's this thing called a split page? You take a piece of paper and fold it in half, and then on one side you write—"

"I'm not learning disabled," Duncan interrupted. Against my will, I imagined him writing, *I do note want too tok abowt this.*

I thought back to my training. "Some people go their whole lives without being diagnosed. And they think they're stupid and they have all kinds of, like, self-esteem issues. But they're not stupid at all. It's just they have this problem with the wiring in their brains. So stuff gets jumbled sometimes, like maybe you're looking at the word 'dog,' but your brain tells you you're seeing—"

"*I am not learning disabled.*"

"'God,'" I said.

"I'm not!"

"No," I explained. "'God' is what you think you see when you read the word 'dog.'"

He stopped on the sidewalk. "Dog: D-o-g. God: G-o-d."

"That doesn't prove anything," I said.

He sighed and closed his eyes. "I have been evaluated by"—he opened his eyes and looked at the night sky, counting—"four special ed people. No, wait. Five. That I can think of. And you know what they figured out?" He turned to face me. "I. Am not. Learning disabled."

"Oh." I crossed my arms over my chest. Against my will, I thought, *So, that means you're just stupid?*

"I never should have left you a note," he said, resuming his walk.

I blushed with shame. "Why?" I asked lamely.

He didn't answer, didn't say anything at all until we'd almost reached the grocery store. "It doesn't matter," he said to the night. "I'm going to work on a fishing boat like my dad. When you're out in the middle of the ocean, it doesn't matter whether or not you can do fractions."

Oh, God, he sucked at math, too?

"But what if that doesn't work out? What if you get, I don't know, nerve damage or something, and you can't handle the hooks?"

"Then I'm screwed." He sighed. "But I'm not stupid."

"Of course you're not!" I chirped. I really need to learn to fake things better.

"No, I'm serious," he said. "They tested me for that, too. My

IQ is actually above average." He caught my expression. "You don't have to look so surprised."

"I guess I just don't understand. . . ."

"I've moved a lot," he said. "And sometimes my dad took a while getting me enrolled in school. And sometimes he was working and he thought I was in school but I was caught up in doing something more important. Like sleeping. And sometimes I went to school but just didn't go to class." We'd reached a big blue mailbox. He leaned against it. "There's just no point anymore. I'm too far behind."

A strange feeling surged through me. Hope? Sympathy? I couldn't quite identify it. "I can help you! We can work together, get you caught up."

"Delilah already tried it," he said.

"For how long?"

"I don't know. A couple of weeks? She gave up."

"I wouldn't give up."

"If you want," he mumbled. "But I don't even know how much longer I'll be living here."

I froze. How ironic if I moved here just as Duncan left. How sad.

"We'll just have to work fast then," I said.

If he moved, I'd deal with it. I'd just have to make the most of whatever time we had left together. And after that—what? Maybe I could tutor some other kids.

"Is there any kind of peer leadership program at your high school?" I asked. "Or student-to-student tutoring?"

He lifted his shoulders. "Don't think so."

"There should be," I said. "There was a whole group of us at

168

my old school. I really think we made a difference."

"Maybe you can start a new program," Duncan said softly.

"That's what I was just thinking!"

He kept his eyes on the ground. "That would look really good on your college application." He had a new edge to his voice.

"That's not why I—" I swallowed. "I just want to help you."

Whatever warm feeling had surged through me was gone now. We walked in silence the rest of the way. His hands stayed in his pockets. If he tried to kiss me good night, I'd let him. I wouldn't even ask his real name.

But he didn't try to kiss me. He didn't even try to shake my hand.

"See ya 'round," he said. And then he was gone.

20.

AFTER ROLF, YOU WOULDN'T THINK I'd be surprised when hot turned cold suddenly and without warning, like when you're standing in a steamy shower and someone flushes the toilet next door. Okay, that's going from cold to hot, but you know what I mean.

I tried to slip into the dark motel room without being heard, but my mother was sitting up in bed, waiting for me. "I know your curfew used to be midnight and it's only eleven fifty, but—"

"If you want to be able to track me down every second of the day, get me a cell phone," I interrupted. I fished my camera out of my top drawer and retreated to the patio, which was the only place besides the bathroom that offered any privacy. At that moment, I'd forgive Lexie's betrayal if only she'd let me share her big house. That would show Duncan. I couldn't believe the way he'd pulled away from me. It wasn't my fault he couldn't spell. You'd think he'd give me some credit for being able to look beyond that.

It was bright on the patio. The lights were on timers. They'd shut off soon.

The camera, warm in my hands, chimed to life. Even with the patio light, the pictures on the little screen were easier to see than they'd been in daytime, the colors richer, the details more distinct. It didn't take long to find the window shot. There were the table and chairs, the painted trim. Outside was a shadowy tree branch, a hint of fog-touched sky. There was Ronald Young, grinning through the pane like a shining angel.

A ray of sunlight: that was Larry's explanation. And yes, it was weird to have something bad happen to Ronald Young after Francine Lunardi's death, but coincidences happen—as do lapses of attention. He was there and I just didn't notice him. It was the only thing that made sense.

The row of patio lights shut off with a loud click. The night was black, the moon covered with dense clouds. My camera screen glowed like a handful of embers, the colors sharper than ever without any surrounding light to dilute them. And that's when I saw it: Ronald Young wasn't simply brighter than the rest of the photograph, as if he were lit from within. Surrounding his slightly fuzzy edges was faint bluish light so subtle that it hadn't shown up on the printed picture.

Blood rushing in my ears, I thumbed back to the shot of Mrs. Lunardi in her pink bathrobe. Sure enough, she, too, had a fuzzy blue halo clinging to every edge.

The night swirled around me. People don't give off blue light. Ronald Young hadn't been a Peeping Tom any more than Francine Lunardi had strolled past me in her slippers.

What was going on? Had my camera foreseen their misfortune—or did it somehow cause it? Mrs. Lunardi had been ill for years; my camera had nothing to do with her death. But what about Ronald Young? If not for that truck, he'd be fine.

I couldn't handle this on my own. I bolted back into the room and out the front door, ignoring my mother's "Where are you going?"

From the parking lot, I scanned the road for Duncan. There was no sign of him. I hurried across the asphalt and onto the sidewalk. The streets seemed darker than when Duncan had walked me home, and the air was just as cold—especially without Duncan's brown sweatshirt to keep me warm. My flip-flops slowed me down. I traveled half a block toward town before realizing that Duncan would have been heading in the opposite direction: away from the ocean, toward the Valley View apartments.

I retreated back to Home Suite Home and continued past it, following the sidewalk to a murky tunnel under the freeway. Around me, the walls shook from cars passing overhead. The smell of urine burned my nose. I scurried through as quickly as I could, but when I emerged on the other side, the night sky seemed even blacker. Trees hung low, and clouds swallowed the moon.

At a fork in the road, I tried to remember which direction we'd taken to see the apartments. Did I even want to go there? The complex had been creepy in the daylight; at night it could be dangerous. Besides, I didn't even know Duncan's apartment number.

I paused on the cracked sidewalk, heart pounding, palms sweating. In my pocket, the camera sat warm and heavy, like something alive. What would happen if I snapped a picture here, on this deserted street? Would someone new turn up? I slid the silver camera out of my pocket and turned it on, its chime tinny in the hushed air. Aiming for nothing but darkness, I clicked the shutter: nothing. Next, I snapped the cloud-covered moon, and at the mouth of the underpass I captured the silhouette of a tree. After each picture, I checked the screen, but there were no figures, no faces, only the sad shapes of a gloomy night.

On my way back through the underpass, I held my breath and tried to ignore the scratching sounds of small creatures scurrying around. By the time I reached the other side, the murky clouds had traveled beyond the almost-full moon, which lit up the sky like an enormous night-light. My pulse slowed. I sighed with relief. I aimed my camera at the man in the moon and snapped a picture as a gesture of appreciation.

My mother was sitting up in bed. "We'll get you a cell phone. But you need to be home by midnight."

"Okay," I said, as if I were giving her permission. And then, after a pause: "Sorry."

"Me too," she whispered.

I zipped my hot camera back into its case and placed it on the kitchen table. I didn't want it too close to me while I slept.

When I woke up the next morning, the camera was gone. Okay, truth: it was afternoon. But the camera was really gone. For a single, sweaty moment I thought it had been spirited away, but my mother, seeing my panicked expression, said, "Your dad took the camera. He wanted to take some pictures of the work site."

"But I need it!" I croaked.

"*He* needs it," my mother corrected, putting her empty coffee mug in the little stainless steel sink. "They're having problems building a retaining wall, and your father had some ideas." She looked me in the eye. "This could be a big deal for him."

"What? He could be promoted from ditchdigger to wall builder?"

I regretted the words as soon as they were out (though my mother should have known better than to speak to me before I'd had my coffee). The crease between her eyebrows deepened to a near-canyon. "This is difficult for all of us."

"My camera is the only thing I have left!"

"That's more than I have," she said.

I was about to say she had about twenty ceramic roosters in a storage unit in Amerige, but I held it in, asking instead, "Where's Dad's job site? Because maybe I could walk down there, and if he's done taking his pictures, I could get my camera back."

"No." For added emphasis, she said it like it had two syllables: No-wah.

Aargh. I really wanted to show Delilah the blue lights, but there was no point arguing with my mother when she was like this. Actually, there was no point arguing with my mother most of the time.

She was dressed in regular clothes: a pale blue polo shirt, khaki shorts, and bright white sneakers. My mother cleans her sneakers in the washing machine.

"Aren't you working today?"

"It's my day off," she said, her eyes narrowing. "I hope that's okay with you."

There was no way I was going to hang around that room. I put on my bathing suit and headed for Psychic Photo.

* * *

174

Delilah wasn't in the shop. Instead, Rose flitted around the room, arranging things on the shelves. There was a new crystals section, I noticed, right next to a photo album display.

"Hi, Madison." Rose smiled as if she had been expecting me. In a simple white sundress, with her auburn haired pulled back in a tidy clip, she looked almost old enough to be a mom. Her ears, neck, and hands were free of jewelry, but she made up for it with an anklet and four silver toe rings.

"Going to the beach?" she asked.

For a moment, it freaked me out that she knew that without being told—but then I realized that my board shorts, bikini top, and beach bag may have tipped her off.

"Uh-huh. I thought Delilah might want to come with."

"She's not big on the beach—burns too easily—but you can ask." She gestured toward the back of the shop, which led to the stairs.

At the doorway I paused. "Did Delilah tell you that we figured out who the guy in the window picture was?"

"Leo did." Her mouth twisted. "Delilah doesn't like to encourage me. At least Larry can calm down now that he knows that guy won't be hanging around."

"Isn't it kind of a weird coincidence?" I said. "You know, that he got hurt right after showing up in my camera? And that Mrs. Lunardi died?"

"Yes," she admitted. "But coincidences happen. In my business, you have to admit that. Otherwise, people won't ever believe you."

"But what if the lighting was weird in both pictures, like something I've never seen before? What if Francine Lunardi and Ronald Young both kind of . . . glowed?"

175

"Larry thinks it's just sunlight. He's probably right."

"It's more than that," I said, dropping the bomb. "I couldn't see it until I looked at my camera in the darkness, but the figures are surrounded by a blue light."

She froze for a moment before asking, "Both of them?"

I nodded and took a deep breath. "Francine Lunardi and Ronald Young weren't there when I took the pictures. I'm positive. There's something going on."

She didn't say anything at first. And honestly? She didn't look all that surprised by what I'd said. Something flickered behind her eyes. "Do you want to tell Delilah or should I?"

It wasn't an easy sell.

"It was late morning. The sun was overhead." Delilah sat on the couch in her apartment, knees drawn up to her chest.

"It's about the same time now," I said, pointing to the window permanently shadowed by a cramped tree and the inn next door. "You see anything but shadows?"

She chewed her freckly lip. "Maybe the flash went off."

"Then it would have reflected against the pane," I said calmly. "And anyway, it wouldn't have turned their edges blue."

"Where's the camera?"

"My dad has it."

Oh, God. What if he deleted the pictures by accident? Then Delilah would never believe me. I was tempted to dash over to my dad's work site and reclaim the little Canon, but if my mother found out, she'd kill me.

Delilah caught me looking around the room. "He's not here."

"Huh?" I said.

176

"Duncan," she said. "He went out on the boat with his father this morning."

"Oh," I said. "Whatever."

Footsteps sounded on the steps outside the apartment.

"Energy," Rose said, bursting in.

"Who's watching the shop?" Delilah demanded.

Rose waved at the air. "We can leave it for a couple of minutes." She plopped down on the floor and pretzeled her legs into what I think is called the Lotus position.

"Please don't launch into your energy routine," Delilah moaned.

"What energy routine?" I asked.

Rose took a deep breath before speaking, her hands moving like a hula dancer's. "There's electric and magnetic energy all around us. We can't see it. Sometimes we feel it, but we attribute it to something else: a breeze, a virus, a cold front. In my work, I tune in to this energy, try to make some sense of it."

"Can we just cut to the photo?" Delilah snapped.

Rose ignored her. "Sometimes energy trumps time and space. Time folds in on itself, and if you tap into the right energy and the right place, you can—"

"Don't say it," Delilah moaned.

"So you think my camera is giving off energy?" I tried. "Making things happen?"

"No." Hands on knees, chin tilted up, she paused for a moment before continuing. "I think it's just really . . . sensitive. I think it's picking up on energy that people—even sensitive ones like myself—can't detect." She looked me straight in the eye. "I think your camera is seeing the future."

"Her camera cannot see the future!" Delilah insisted, but she sounded more frightened than assured.

"It's seeing something," Rose said.

"I've had the camera for two years, and nothing strange ever happened before the repair," I said.

"It wasn't the repair," Rose said. "It was the energy. The forces in the back room were off the charts the day you dropped off your camera. A night immersed in that kind of electromagnetism must have sharpened your camera's sensitivities."

"But what if it happens again? What if someone else shows up?" I asked, suddenly afraid to take any more pictures. "Do I try to find the person? Do I warn them?"

"You have to," Delilah said.

"I thought you didn't believe in this stuff," I said. It came out wrong, like an accusation. In truth, I wanted Delilah to remain skeptical, to tell me the world made sense. It was one thing when I thought my little Canon could see ghosts. That was kind of fun. Now it had turned into an electronic Grim Reaper, and it was really starting to scare me.

"It wouldn't do any good," Rose said from the floor. "The past, the present, the future—they're too intertwined. You can't stop the future because it's already happened."

Delilah wasn't nearly as creeped out as I was. "You need to know that my mother is infantile, egocentric, and deluded," she said, twisting the pole of her beach umbrella into the sand. She'd dressed for the beach in knee-length board shorts, a long-sleeve rash guard shirt, and a wide-brimmed straw hat. I'd never seen someone expose so little skin at the beach. It was like she was Amish or something.

I rummaged through my beach bag and pulled out a bottle of store-brand sunscreen. "What your mom said made sense, though, didn't it?"

"No." She popped up the umbrella. "That energy stuff is ridiculous." She tilted her pale, freckled chin toward the sky and sighed with frustration. "I wish I could just sit in the sun like a normal person."

"If your mom's wrong, why is this happening?" I pressed.

She pulled an enormous pair of round white sunglasses out of her straw beach bag and slipped them on. "Your camera's haunted. It's the only thing that makes any sense." She peered over the glasses. "But don't tell my mother I said that."

We spent a surprisingly normal day at the beach. Delilah sat hunched under the umbrella while I baked on the bright warm sand. The store-brand lotion left white streaks on my body, but it smelled nice, like pineapples.

When my fingers began to swell from the heat, Delilah smeared her exposed bits with an additional layer of SPF a gazillion sunblock, and we headed for the water. I made it to my waist in the icy froth before I stopped, jumping and shrieking as the waves hit my chest. Delilah pushed ahead and dove under a breaker. She swam a few strokes out and motioned me to follow. I held out my arms for balance and shook my head: this was as far as I wanted to go.

She caught a tiny wave and swam back to me. "When the water's this cold, you've just got to dive in and keep swimming until it doesn't hurt anymore."

I shook my head. "I mostly swim in pools. It's not like I've never been in the ocean, but . . ." I had been about to say that the water was a lot warmer in the Caribbean when I realized how obnoxious that sounded. Above us, the sky was bright blue, but angry clouds darkened the horizon. I thought of Duncan out on the fishing boat.

"You can swim, right?" Delilah asked.

"Yeah," I said. "Of course." The waves really weren't that bad, but the current tugged at my legs.

"Follow me." She pointed to a yellow float way out, bobbing in the waves. "It's really calm out there." Beyond us, the float lurched on a swell.

A wave slammed into my chest and splattered my face. I stumbled backward.

Delilah caught my arm to steady me. "Come on." She plunged into the water and swam away with choppy strokes.

When an oversized wave charged toward me, I had no choice but to dive under. Soon, I was beyond the breakers. I swam with my head above the surface until I caught up with Delilah, treading water.

"See?" she said. "Just like a big swimming pool."

It was nothing like a swimming pool. The water was dark and unpredictable, and the currents did everything they could to pull me off course. My legs disappeared in the churning water below me; the ocean floor could be two feet down or twenty. It could be dotted with sand dollars or swirling with eels. Anxious, I scanned the choppy surface for fins. I never should have watched "Shark Week."

When we finally reached the swim float, I hauled myself up,

panting from exertion and fear. From here, the sunny shore didn't seem so far away, but the horizon had grown even blacker, turning the water at the edge of the earth a steely gray. Wind blew in violent gusts. Goose bumps rose on my wet flesh.

"How far out was Duncan going?" I asked.

"Pretty far, I think," Delilah said. "No one booked the boat for today, so they can stay out as long as they want." When she saw my expression, she added, "The boat has radar. When they see there's a storm, they'll either steer around it or come back early. Rain is no big deal."

A bunch of little kids dangled from the float, splashing and laughing. A couple couldn't have been older than eight, which made me feel like a major wimp for being scared. There were some teenagers in red bathing suits sprawled around, too, including the gorgeous blond guy who'd made Delilah blush last week.

"Hey, Nate," Delilah said. "You doing the lifeguard thing?"

He grinned, and dimples sprouted in his tanned cheeks. "Sea guard camp; I'm a junior counselor. We're done for the day, though, so I figured I'd come out here and hang." He squinted at the dark horizon. "Looks like a storm's coming, though."

Delilah smiled. She nodded. She blushed and stared—speechless for once. I turned away and covered my mouth so she wouldn't see me laughing.

Back on shore, we wrapped ourselves in towels and pulled down Delilah's beach umbrella so the wind wouldn't carry it off.

"So I guess you like that guy," I said.

"Who?" she asked, all innocent.

I snorted with laughter; she knew exactly who I was talking about.

"Of course I like him," she admitted.

"It seemed mutual."

"Nah." She rolled her eyes. "He's nice to everybody. Nate's completely out of my league—which is the point, really. I don't plan to date until I'm thirty."

I raised my eyebrows. "Thirty?"

"Maybe twenty-nine. If I meet someone really special." She shot me a half grin before slipping on her big sunglasses. The sun still glared, even as the clouds took over the sky. "Before I get involved with anybody, I've got to finish high school, go to college, establish a career, and pay off my student loans. I can't risk any distractions." It was almost as if she were talking to herself, convincing herself.

She angled herself toward the water. "My mother had Leo when she was fifteen, and she had me a year and a half later." She turned her head. "By two different fathers."

I tried not to look shocked. I failed.

"Duncan didn't tell you?" she said.

"Just how old she was. I guess I just assumed—"

"That it was one guy? Nope. Though she was in *love*"—she held up her fingers to indicate quotation marks—"so it was okay. Leo's father was on the football team—which, when you think about Leo, is actually pretty funny. He dumped her as soon as she got pregnant. And then his parents moved out of state, which was really convenient for them."

"And your father?"

"Valedictorian of the class. If you can believe it."

I looked at Delilah: genetics in action. "I can believe it."

She shook her head. "You wouldn't think someone so smart would be stupid enough to get his girlfriend pregnant. My mother thought he was her Einstein in shining armor—you know, asking her out even though she had a baby. And he did stick with her after I was born—for almost a year, I think. But he said it would be better for them both if he got an education. So he left. And I guess he just forgot to come back."

Out in the water, the last kids abandoned the float and made for shore.

"And now?"

"He's an architect. Lives in Seattle with his wife and their two children. Max and Sophia. A boy and a girl—just like us." So I wasn't the only one around here living life in a parallel universe.

Around us, moms pulled sweatshirts over toddlers' heads while dads gathered towels and trash. Delilah and I stayed planted on the sand.

"Do you see him?" I pressed. "Does he send money or anything?"

She shook her head violently. I thought of her eBay business, her long work hours, her cramped apartment.

"But he should. He's your father."

"No, he's not. He's just some guy." She exhaled with frustration. "And the thing about my mother? She threw herself at those boys—just like she threw herself at lots of guys after them. None of them even cared about her. And now she's got Larry, who'd do anything for her—he'd do anything for Leo and me—and she's just pushing him away. She says he can't stay in one place, but he's already said he'll stay if she marries him. Her real problem?

183

She refuses to grow up. If she gets married, it means she isn't a kid anymore." Her voice grew wobbly. "She doesn't even think about what the rest of us want."

"Do you think Larry and Duncan are going to leave?" I asked, hoping she'd say no.

She reached under her sunglasses to rub her eye. "If she doesn't come to her senses, then, yeah—they'll leave. Duncan knows he can stay with us. But I think he's afraid that if he doesn't go with Larry, he'll never see him again."

The rain started quickly, angrily, the fat drops like punches on our skin. We stuffed our things into our beach bags and hurried up the street.

At Psychic Photo, Leonardo sat behind the counter, eyes closed, chin tilted up, listening to a portable CD player. When he heard the door, he yanked off his headphones, popped off the stool, and made for the front door. "Mom's in the back, doing a reading for a new client. Thanks for taking over for me, Dee. I've got some stuff I need to do. Hi, Madison; see you later."

He disappeared into the rain before Delilah could say, "But I need to change my clothes!"

"You want me to hang down here while you shower?" I asked.

"Nah. My mom should be out soon."

I expected Rose to emerge from the back room with a chattering, flowered-dress type like Mrs. Voorhees, someone who'd gush about energy and karma and transformation. Instead the woman who shuffled out a few minutes later had a tearstained face and sagging shoulders. She wore jean shorts and a blue T-shirt. Her blond hair hung limp around her face.

184

"I just wish I'd known earlier," she told Rose. "I would have shown him more patience. More understanding."

"It's not too late," Rose said. "Go to him. Let him feel your energy, your love. You can make your connection in this life even stronger than it was in the last."

Delilah's face turned so red it was practically purple. When the blond woman left the store, she exploded, "You don't do past-life regressions, remember?"

Rose spoke quietly. "This was a special case."

"Who was she in a former life—Queen Elizabeth? Betsy Ross? Have you ever noticed that only famous people get reincarnated? Why don't slaves and peasants ever get a second chance?"

"This wasn't about fame," Rose said. "It was about Jennifer's relationship with her husband. He's always acted so helpless around her. She thought it might have been her fault, something she was doing, but I helped her see that their dynamics were the result of a previous relationship."

"They were married in another life?" Delilah ventured.

Rose shook her head. "Her husband . . . was her son."

"Ew!" Delilah and I said at the same time—and then we burst into laughter.

"It's not funny!" Rose snapped, silencing us with her ferocity. "They've brought another soul into their marriage: she's going to have a baby. And that realization changed her husband in a fundamental way. She didn't come here to talk about past lives but to learn about her future. Her husband is in a coma. She wanted me to tell her if he would live or die."

"No," Delilah whispered.

Rose nodded. "Jennifer is Ronald Young's wife. The doctors

185

had hoped he'd regain consciousness by now. It doesn't look good."

Of course: Delilah and I had seen the woman before, when she came to help her husband at the photo printer.

"So what did you tell her?" Delilah asked.

Rose raised her shoulders. "That I didn't know what would happen. I tried to look ahead, but I couldn't see anything. So I told her what I sensed about their past relationship. And I told her to love him. That was the best I could do."

Delilah stood in the front doorway with me. The rain hadn't let up, but I was already drenched; a little more water wouldn't make any difference.

"You going to be around later?" I asked.

"Yeah."

"If it stops raining, I'll come back with my camera. You've really got to look at those photos again."

I expected Delilah to say something about Ronald Young's wife. Instead, she crossed her arms and looked at her feet. "Don't hurt Duncan. He's been through a lot already."

I tried to answer, but the words wouldn't come out.

"Don't drip all over the carpet," my mother said when I burst into the room, soaked and bedraggled from ocean, wind, and rain.

"Where's dad?"

"In the shower."

"Do you know where he put my camera?" Oh, God, what if he'd gotten it wet?

"You can ask him when he comes out." She took a clean pot

from the drying rack and put it in the cabinet with a clang. "Lexie called," she added casually.

I felt like I'd been hit. "How did she know where we were staying?"

"She called my cell phone." With some more clattering she put away the rest of the dishes. "You want to call her back?"

I didn't answer.

"Madison?" She turned to see if I'd heard her.

"Maybe later," I said.

Suddenly, the room shook with an enormous boom. I yelped.

"Just thunder," my mother said. "Better get used to it if we're going to live here."

I sat on the couch and waited for my mother to tell me not to sit on the couch in a wet bathing suit. Astonishingly, she didn't.

"What did Lexie say?" I mumbled.

"She said, 'Is Madison there?'"

"Thanks," I said. "That's helpful."

The thunder boomed again, louder this time, as my father, wearing a plain white T-shirt and gray sweatpants, emerged from the bathroom rubbing his hair with a towel.

"Did you hear the news?" he asked.

"Yeah," I said, thinking he meant Lexie's call.

"Things are looking good," he said, standing straighter than he had in some time.

"Huh?"

"And there's plenty of room for growth." He chucked the towel back through the open bathroom door.

"I have no idea what you're talking about," I said.

"Your father got a promotion," my mother said. "Site foreman."

"Great," I said. "Did Lexie say anything else?"

"It's a new project," my father said. "A remodel. We'll probably get started in the next week or two. And after that who knows?"

"There's paid vacation time," my mother said. "And in six months, health insurance, even dental." She held my gaze. "This means we're definitely staying in Sandyland. I'll stop by the high school tomorrow, get you enrolled. And we'll start looking harder for someplace to live."

I nodded, accepting the inevitable. It didn't really matter what Lexie had said.

"Dad, where's my camera?"

"In my backpack," he said. "In the bathroom."

The camera was buried under a stained, smelly sweatshirt that I tried, unsuccessfully, not to touch. I turned off the overhead light, sat on the edge of the tub, and pressed the power button. There were no windows in the bathroom; with the lights off, it was as black as a moonless night.

First I came across my dad's shots: a ditch, a hill, a cinder-block wall—thrilling stuff. I zipped back until I got to the pictures from Delilah's apartment, afraid of what I might see. If Ronald Young's blue halo had disappeared, everyone would think I had been lying.

But there he was, still rimmed by the ghostly light. I savored relief for only an instant before anxiety took up its now familiar residence in my gut. I examined the other pictures from that day but found nothing out of place.

My mother rapped on the door. "Hurry up. I need to use the restroom." (So formal: just once I'd like to hear my mother say, "I gotta pee.")

"One sec," I said.

In my hands, the shots on the screen followed one another like flashes of lightning. When I got to the pictures I'd taken the night before, a tingle passed through me. The shots around the tunnel were murky, the shadows ominous. Were these pictures really that scary, or was I just projecting my remembered anxiety onto them? I could still hear the scampering of the rats, smell the urine, feel the wind.

When I reached the final shot, my anxiety turned to terror. The moon, freed from the clouds, glowed in the night sky: a shining, happy face edged in blue.

In the sphere I saw two eyes, a nose, a mouth. But the face grinning back at me wasn't the man in the moon.

It was Duncan.

21.

BEYOND PSYCHIC PHOTO'S FRONT DOOR, the printer's lights glowed like fireflies. Behind me the rain fell in needles.

Rose was at the counter. I must have looked like a crazy person, still in my board shorts and bikini top, my hair a mess of salt and rain, my face streaked with tears and snot. But Rose was good with crazy people. She led me to the back room without a word and rummaged through some of Delilah's eBay boxes until she found a blanket. She eased me onto a couch and sat next to me, quiet, waiting.

"Duncan," I said at last.

"He's not here," she said. "They went fishing, but they're probably back by now. The storm—"

"He's in danger!" I sobbed. I couldn't say "dead." Or "dying." Not yet.

She shook her head. "We get these storms all the time. I know it seems scary, but it's not that big a deal."

Her voice was so calm and soothing. As she picked up the phone

190

to call Duncan and Larry's apartment, I almost believed that someone would answer, that everything was going to be okay.

Several seconds passed. I forgot to breathe. Rose shook her head and put down the phone. "I'm sure they're fine."

Tears blurring my vision, I turned on my camera and found the moon shot.

Rose froze, her eyes wide with horror. "No," she whispered.

She grabbed the phone and punched in some numbers; she shut her eyes, her breathing ragged. "Is this the harbormaster? I'm trying to find out about a charter boat, the *Peggy*." She nodded and said, "Right, Ray Clarke's boat. He took it out early this morning, along with Larry Vaughn and his son, Duncan."

Her features clenched in frustration. "I'm not his wife, I'm his—I'm a friend. I don't know where they were planning to go. But I thought they'd be back by now, and—" Her gaze fell on the camera burning hot in my hand.

"Can you radio them?" she pleaded. "Just make sure they're okay?"

When she hung up, she crumpled to the couch next to me and dissolved into tears.

There were footfalls down the back stairs, and the door opened: Delilah. Her face was paler than usual. She looked upset but not surprised—not even a little bit.

"Duncan?" she asked in a small voice.

After I'd shown Delilah the photo; after the harbor patrol had called back to say they'd been unable to make contact with the *Peggy*; after Rose had phoned Larry's friends and neighbors and fellow fishermen and then his home number again—just in case—we piled into Rose's car and headed for Kimberley Cove. Outside, the car was small and gray, scratched and dented. Inside, duct tape held the black vinyl upholstery together. A cardboard Christmas tree, its piney scent long gone, hung from the rearview mirror.

The rain had slowed to a drizzle. Rose set the windshield wipers on the lowest setting. Every time I thought they were off for good, they'd screech an arc across the chipped glass, leaving a half-moon trail of misty dirt.

We didn't talk. When we reached Kimberley Cove, Rose brought the car to a jerky halt, hopped out, and dashed across the small rutted parking lot to the weathered gray shed that was the harbormaster's office.

Delilah and I headed for the pier, longing to see the *Peggy* bouncing over the waves on her way to safety. I checked my camera. Duncan was still there, laughing with the man in the moon.

It was low tide. At the end of the pier, a steep gangplank led to a dock. I clutched the wet, splintery railing and took baby steps, trying not to stumble over my flip-flops.

At the bottom, the dock swayed under my feet. The sky looked like a double exposure: a stormy day overlaid on a sunny one. Rays of sun snuck through the clouds like spotlights among curtains of rain. Had this been a week earlier—or even a day earlier—I would have pulled out my camera and shot the view.

Anchored boats cluttered the harbor, but the *Peggy*'s big round mooring bounced around like a child's abandoned ball. The other vessels lurched on the waves, the sky-high captain's chairs plunging here and there like amusement park rides. Of course, in an amusement park, you'd be strapped in. A picture flashed in my brain: Duncan perched high on the lookout tower, scanning the water for fish, ignoring the waves until a big one launched him off his perch and into the shark-filled sea.

I must have made a sound because Delilah said, "What?"

"Maybe the boat's okay but he fell in the water. From the top."

She held my gaze for a moment, her gray eyes drenched with pain and loss, before turning her stare to the horizon. "Sometimes, before something bad happens—I get a feeling. Not anything specific, just this . . . sense."

"And?" I whispered.

She shook her head. "Nothing."

"But you knew," I said. "When you saw me at the shop, you knew I was there about Duncan."

"I could feel your fear," she said. "That's all."

A few minutes later, wet and shivering, Delilah and I approached the harbormaster's office. Rose stood in the open doorway, letting in the rain.

"Can't you send someone out to look?" she pleaded to the gray-haired man who sat behind a big steel desk.

The harbormaster rubbed his faded blue eyes. "Lady, I'm not that worried. A couple of boats just came in, and they said it wasn't that bad."

"What about the Coast Guard?" Rose pressed. "Can we ask them to look?"

"A family member could call," he said with a shrug.

"We're like family," Rose said.

The harbormaster raised an eyebrow at the "like"—but he called anyway.

"They'll find 'em," he said once he'd hung up. "They'll give me all kinds of grief for sending them out for no reason, but they'll find 'em."

But they didn't. A few agonizing hours later, the sun broke through for real, just in time to splatter the clouds with orange paint. There had been no sign of the *Peggy*. The harbormaster locked the office, muttering that he'd already stayed way past closing time.

"They're probably fine," he told Rose. We all wanted to believe him.

On the wet dock, in our clammy clothes, we watched the sun slip below some more clouds and then pop out again before bumping up against the horizon. We squinted against the orange glare, searching, searching for the boat.

Rose was quiet. Every once in a while she'd close her eyes and whisper, "I'd know if he was hurt."

And maybe Duncan was still alive. Ron Young hadn't died— at least not yet. Maybe we could save Duncan, if only we knew where he was.

When just the faintest rim of pink remained in the dark sky, Delilah spoke. "We should go home."

"But we can't," Rose and I said at the same time.

"If they hear anything, they'll call us. Leo's probably wondering where we are."

As the final color drained from the night sky, I checked the camera one last time, my hands shaking so badly that I released the shutter, snapping a picture of the dark, endless water. I skimmed past my father's construction photos until I reached the picture of Duncan smiling through the moon.

"Don't go," I whispered to him.

I asked Rose to drop me at the beach on the way back. I wasn't ready to go back to the motel room.

Moving across the sand, I felt weirdly disconnected. It was like I was walking on someone else's legs, seeing through someone else's eyes. The ocean was black, sprinkled with moonbeams. A single flip-flop, patterned with flowers, lay half buried in the sand. A line of shells shone like a giant's crooked smile.

How could I feel so miserable when the world was so beautiful? Had it always been this way?

The soaked sand was mushy cold on my feet. The salty air felt damp and alive. The stars shone like pinpricks: so many suns, light-years away. We were so small, really, and our time on earth so short.

I sat on the wet sand and closed my eyes. So what if we didn't have a big house anymore. Now I got to live in a place with sweet air and watercolor sunsets, where ghostly morning fog gave way to golden afternoons. I still had my parents. I had friends. I'd go to school and work hard, and in a few years I'd go to college—there were scholarships. Everything was going to be all right.

Tears soaked my face before I even realized I was crying. Duncan understood. He knew that nothing mattered more than the people you loved. He'd learned to live every day as if it might be his last.

Finally, I got up and brushed the mucky sand off my legs.

Above the sea, the moon, slightly fuzzy, rose above the horizon, dodging between clouds. I'd never again look at the moon without thinking of Duncan, without wondering if he was up there in the sky, looking back at me.

From now on, I'd have to live for both of us.

When I got back to the motel, my parents were lounging on the bed watching a sitcom. They smiled at me absently before returning their attention to the small screen.

I headed for the bathroom. In the shower, no one would hear me cry.

"Lexie phoned again," my mother called out.

I paused in the doorway. "I'll call her tomorrow." I would, too.

When I got out of the shower, my parents were still watching television. Head down, I grabbed my mother's cell phone and my camera and hurried out to the patio, where I collapsed on a white plastic chair and listened to the noises of the night. Funny: I'd never noticed before how much passing traffic sounded like the ocean.

First, I called Psychic Photo, feeling bad when I heard Rose's anxious, "Hello?" I hadn't meant to get her hopes up. Duncan and Larry were still gone.

Next, I turned on my camera, almost afraid of what I might see. Would Larry be in a picture, smiling with his son? Would Ray Clarke, the boat's captain, show up? Rose's clients paid to have their fortunes told. But what good was knowing what was going to happen if there was nothing you could do to change the outcome?

The Canon felt even hotter than usual, like the metal could burn my palms. I zipped to the moon photo, a final spark of hope still simmering in my chest. And then the spark went out. Duncan was still there, trapped in the small screen, cursed by the moon.

I checked the construction shots again, just in case. Duncan being Duncan, he could have snuck into a different frame. He could be playing with shovels, digging in the dirt. But he wasn't there.

There was a picture I hadn't seen: the snap I'd taken on the pier, when my shaking hands had accidentally released the shutter. It was the kind of poorly lit, blurry mistake I'd normally delete without a second glance. When I'd pushed the button, there was nothing in front of the lens but dark, choppy sea.

But my camera had seen something else. Just under the surface of the water, a person floated, arms and legs spread out like a starfish, wide eyes staring up at the sky.

It wasn't Duncan. It wasn't Larry. And it wasn't Ray Clarke.

It was me.

22.

I DIDN'T CRY. I DIDN'T SCREAM. It's almost like I was expecting to see myself in the camera. *So this is where the story ends.*

I turned it off and laid it in my lap. It burned my bare legs, but I didn't move it.

My mother slid open the glass door. "It's late. You should come in."

I didn't answer. There were so many things I wanted to say to her, but none of them would make things right.

"Did you hear me?"

"Soon."

I should tell her I love her.

She slid the door closed.

This is where it ends.

Sleep eluded me. I lay on my back on the scratchy couch, tears sliding silently into my ears. I cried for myself: the things I'd never do, the people I'd never meet. I cried for sweet, lost Duncan. I cried for the foolish girl I used to be. I cried for my parents and the pain this would cause them. I cried for Lexie, who I'd never see again.

How would it happen? The possibilities jostled my brain: a rogue car jumping the curb. A piece of hot dog caught in my windpipe. A carbon monoxide leak, a stray bullet, a meteorite. There were so many ways to die. Maybe I'd just drown, like Duncan probably did. They say it doesn't hurt. Maybe I'd go into a coma like Ronald Young. Had he regained consciousness yet? Somehow I knew that he hadn't.

Sometime after four A.M. I gave up on sleep. I got off the couch and tiptoed through the room, pausing to study my sleeping parents. Were they dreaming of our old house? Or of carnations and ditches?

My mom's cell phone in hand, I slid open the glass door and went out to the patio. For a moment, my heart raced as I imagined a knife-wielding psychopath popping out of the darkness. But then I thought, *No. I will not let fear rule the rest of my day. The rest of my life.* Were they the same thing?

I wouldn't normally call Lexie—or anyone—in the middle of the night, but I had to make things right before time ran out.

The phone rang four times before going to voice mail. I hung up and hit the number again. And again. After five tries, she finally picked up.

"*Madison?*" she croaked.

"Hey." I hadn't actually figured out what I was going to say.

Suddenly, she sounded very awake. "I called you earlier—did your mom tell you?"

"Yeah."

Her words tumbled out. "I needed to tell you that I feel, like, so unbelievably bad about what happened—you know, with Rolf and everything. He's an awesome guy and I really like him, but your friendship means more than anything. If the only way we can stay friends is if I break up with him, I'll do it—I swear. I told him that tonight and he was bummed, but it doesn't matter. You're my best friend, and I need to know that you don't hate me." Her voice cracked.

On the other side of the hill, a truck rumbled by. A few doors down, a baby began to wail.

I said, "Of course I don't hate you. We'll be best friends . . . for the rest of our lives. And Rolf . . ." I tried to remember why I ever thought he mattered. "I don't care if you go out with him. I mean, I think he's kind of a jerk, so be careful. But if you want to give it a shot, go ahead."

"Celia's being a total cow," Lexie said. "Telling everyone that I stole him from her, which is so not true. She even called Melissa to say that . . ."

My attention wavered. I thought of Delilah and her crazy clothes and her funky art. I thought of Leo's disco ball.

". . . and so I can, like, talk to my mom," Lexie said.

"Huh?"

"I don't think she'd let you move in with us forever, but maybe for a few months. Do you think that would give your parents enough time to figure things out?"

"You want me to move in with you?" I said, surprised.

"No guarantees, but I can ask."

"Thanks," I said. "But—I'm happy here. I have friends, and I have . . ." Should I say it? Oh, why not. I'd be with him soon enough. "I have a boyfriend."

200

"Ohmigod! You gotta tell me!"

"Later, maybe," I said. "The sun will be up soon. I think I'll hit the beach."

When my parents woke up, they'd find a note on the little kitchen table.

Mom & Dad—
Off to take some pics at the beach. It's going to be a
beautiful day.
Madison
P.S. I love you both.

With luck, I'd come back from the beach unharmed. But I was going to catch a final sunrise, even if it killed me.

The alley behind Psychic Photo was shadowy. Something skittered and I jumped, but it was just some animal (a cat, I told myself, even as I suspected that the "c" should be an "r"). I placed four plastic grocery bags next to the purple back door, trying to keep the rustling to a minimum. There was no need to wake Delilah. There were no wrongs to right between us, nothing to explain. In some ways, she understood me better than anyone.

The bags were stuffed with my old clothes. They were kind of worn, but they were all good brands. I'd even put my new swimsuit and my Seven jeans in there. They wouldn't do me any good where I was going. I hoped Delilah would keep some of the clothes for herself instead of selling everything on eBay. But the decision was hers to make, as she'd understand from the short note I'd stuffed into one of the bags.

Deliah—
All yours.
Madison

As for me, I was wearing my old black shorts and the pink-and-black T-shirt. My mother had finally washed them.

I checked the parking spot in front of the shop: no motorcycle. I hiked over to Kimberley Cove and checked the mooring: no boat.

By the time I got to the beach, the sky had lightened, but the water was still calm and silvery, the shadows long, the post-storm clouds a watercolor pink. The clouds were drifting away already, leaving a clean, sharp, blue sky. For once, there was no fog.

It seemed pointless, in a way, to take pictures. My camera couldn't stop time or save me. A photograph isn't real life. It's just what we think we see.

But right now, instead of coming between me and the world, the camera brought us closer. It allowed me to really see the beauty around me—not just in the shapes and the shadows, but in the things that were actually there: the sand and the seaweed, the water and the rocks. There were birds and seals and the occasional human being.

There was beauty in other things: a torn volleyball net, spider-web cracks on the sidewalk, Delilah's favorite trash cans. You just needed to look harder to recognize the wonder of the shadows, the miracle of the shapes.

It made me feel better to know that the world would go on without me, even as I ached to realize how much I was losing. A breeze kissed my cheek, and I thought: *Duncan*. His spirit was all around me, in the cool morning air, in the coarse sand, in the sound of the waves.

Was Duncan looking down on me now? My family had never been big on religion, but I suddenly felt sure that death wasn't the end. There had to be something more, something that comes after. There had to be a piece of Duncan and a part of me that would live forever.

When the first beachgoers showed up, lugging coolers and beach bags, chairs and umbrellas, I pushed myself off the sand. At the water's edge I let the cold froth lick my toes. Something glinted in a wave. I reached down and pulled out a sand dollar. Duncan said they brought good luck. I tossed the shell back into the waves for someone else to find.

As I walked away, I once again felt that peculiar sensation, as if I were seeing the world with someone else's eyes. In the parking lot, deliciously greasy smells were already pouring out of the white-and-blue snack shack. If I lived until lunch, I'd come back for a cheeseburger. I passed the ice cream store where Ron Young had bought his last sorbet and a burrito shop that Delilah said was the best. Soon I reached the surf shop. Had that green-and-white bathing suit really mattered in the end? Had it really made me any happier?

Well, yeah. That suit was awesome. In fact, the very thought of the green diagonal stripe on the board shorts made me smile through my pain.

* * *

I made it back to the motel without any problem. My father was finishing his cereal, and my mother was tucking her green polo work shirt into her black pants.

Tears blurred my vision. "I love you guys!"

They stared at me like I was a total nut job.

"We love you, too, honey," my dad said, blinking away tears of his own.

"Is everything okay?" my mother asked.

"Yeah. It's fine. I just— Yeah."

"We have wonderful news," my mother said. Her eyes were shining, happy. I tried to remember the last time she'd looked like this.

"You know that funeral I did recently?" she said. "Francine Lunardi?"

My stomach clenched. "Kinda."

"I just got off the phone with her daughter. Mrs. Lunardi owned a little cottage: two bedrooms, one and a half baths. Not big, but just two blocks from the beach. She left it to her daughter, but the daughter wants to wait until the market picks back up before she sells it. Besides, the cottage needs a lot of work."

I nodded, trying to follow. "And she wants Dad to be the contractor?" I wanted to know that they'd be okay.

My mother shook her head. "Even better: She's going to let us live there—free! For two years, at the very least. In return Daddy will renovate it, but she'll pay for all the materials. We're on our way to see it now—will you come?"

I was so tired, it felt like someone had tied a big band around my forehead. But I liked the idea of knowing where my parents were in case I got the chance to look down on them.

204

Mrs. Lunardi's yellow cottage looked like something out of a storybook (a happy storybook—nothing with witches or trolls). It had a white picket fence and an overgrown rose garden. A blue front door opened into a boxy living room with a brick fireplace and wide-plank, scratched wood floors. There was a kitchen with black and white checkerboard tiles, a bathroom with a claw-foot bathtub, and two tiny bedrooms under a sloping roof.

"First thing I'd do is bump out the back of the house and add a master suite," my dad told Joanne Torres, Francine Lunardi's daughter. "Then right away you're up to a three-bed, two-bath house—much better for resale."

We all sat at the kitchen table so my parents and Mrs. Torres could sign papers. Mrs. Torres was older than I expected, with gray roots in her one-tone brown hair, and sad lines around her mouth.

"The house is darling," my mother said, visions of flowered curtains and shabby-chic furniture probably swimming in her head. "I can see why you might want to move back here sometime."

Mrs. Torres shook her head. "It's not that. It's just—this house meant so much to my mother, I'm not ready to let it go."

She chewed on her lip before continuing. "My mother and I didn't talk for over twenty-five years. It was my fault. I was . . . a bad kid. Alcohol and drugs, and . . . I stole things. But my mother kept forgiving me, over and over, until . . ." Her voice drifted off.

"You must miss her," my mother said.

Mrs. Torres nodded, eyes tearing. "I stole her engagement ring," she blurted. "When I was nineteen. My dad had just died. I pawned the ring and we couldn't get it back."

My father looked at his watch. My mother covered her ring.

Mrs. Torres cleared her throat. "I grew up, cleaned up my act, but my mother just couldn't get past it. And then, a couple of weeks ago, it was like someone had flipped a switch. She called to say she forgave me—and she hoped I could forgive her. I flew out here right away, and we had the most amazing couple of days. It was like we were starting over."

My mother didn't know what to say. My father, who hates this kind of touchy-feely stuff, said, "I promise you I'll do a nice job on the house." And, "I should really be getting back to the job site."

I sat rooted to the heavy wood chair, wishing Mrs. Torres would explain why a person had to face death in order to have the kind of wisdom that had come at last to Francine Lunardi—and now to me.

We dropped my father off at the construction site. "Okay if I borrow your camera again, Maddy?" he asked, getting out of the car.

I hesitated. What would he think if he saw the picture of me floating in the water? But then I decided it was okay. Maybe he could make sense of it someday.

"Let me check one thing." My black hair hung over the screen like a privacy curtain as I looked at the dark water picture. I was still there, floating like a starfish just under the surface, my eyes round as sand dollars.

I turned off the camera and handed it to my dad. "Keep it as long as you like."

My mother left me at the motel and then went off to do some errands. I longed to sink onto the big brown bed, but I couldn't be sure I'd wake up. It would be four days before my parents could move into the yellow cottage. Risking death in their bed just seemed inconsiderate.

As I settled myself onto the couch, I wished I'd worn nicer clothes. If it was my time to leave this earth, I'd rather do it in something other than my Goth Girl getup. But as I drifted off to sleep, I realized that it didn't really matter.

23.

HIS BREATH, COLD AND MINTY, woke me up. "Charles," he whispered.

I opened my eyes and saw Duncan's face, the light behind him so bright I had to squint. I felt safe, not afraid at all. From now on, everything would be okay.

He smiled, revealing the chip in his tooth. At least that was the same. Otherwise he looked different: his hair was short and his earrings were gone. Was there a dress code in the afterlife?

He leaned forward and put his mouth on mine, his lips cool and gentle. He tasted like peppermint and sweet tea. It was nothing like kissing Rolf. Nothing like anything I'd ever felt before.

So this is why they call it heaven.

He leaned back and smiled, his lips redder now.

"Are we dead?" I whispered.

His mouth dropped open. And then he started laughing, and I sat up on the couch and looked around. Heaven looked just like our room at Home Suite Home in the late afternoon, with a slice of sunlight sneaking through the front window. You'd think God would spring for better carpet.

"You're alive?" I said. "You're not even hurt?"

He spread his arms. "Sure looks that way."

"But—what? How?" I shook my head. "You were in my camera."

"Delilah told me." He sat next to me on the couch and put an arm around my shoulders. "I'm kinda glad I didn't see the picture. It would've freaked me out. Though Ronald Young came out of his coma last night—I heard some people at the pier talking about it."

"He did? Really? But . . . did you almost die?" I asked. "Was the storm bad? Did you fall off the boat or anything?"

He shook his head. "It was no big deal. We just got some rain and wind. And anyway, we were on land the whole time."

I blinked with confusion. He tucked a piece of black hair behind my ear.

"There's this little island," he explained. "South of here and about twenty miles out. It's a nature preserve—you're not even supposed to go onshore unless you have a special permit. Which we didn't. It's a great place to camp: totally deserted and there's tons of fish. We anchored the boat in this little hidden cove and turned off the radio."

"Why?" I remembered Rose's frantic pleas, the harbormaster's attempts at radio contact.

"So no one would know where we were. Then this morning we were hauling in the fish like you wouldn't believe, and a frickin' helicopter flies over!" He began to laugh. "I thought Ray Clarke—you know, the guy who owns the boat—was gonna pee in his pants. Now he's gotta pay all these fines because he didn't have a permit. He's way pissed at Rose."

"What happened to your hair?" I was still not entirely convinced he was alive.

He rolled his green eyes up as if he could see the top of his head. "I did it for you. Well, for your parents, anyway." His eyes shot to the sliding glass door. My father sat out there, facing the hill. He must have let Duncan in.

"But I liked your hair," I said, missing the wild tangles, the touches of blond.

"You did?" He looked surprised. "I can always grow it back. It's just hair."

"What about your earrings?"

"They're in my pocket."

"Good." I had one more question. "Who's Charles?"

"I am," he said simply.

I shook my head. "But there's nothing wrong with that name. Why don't you want anyone to know it?"

He took a deep breath. "Can't we just go back to kissing?"

"Soon. But first I want to hear about Charles."

Duncan's mother named him Charles after her own father, who let her move in with him when she got pregnant.

"I think it was just easier than coming up with a new name," Duncan said. "She'd gone out with my dad for a couple of months, but they'd already split up. He didn't even know about me."

She wasn't the worst mother in the world. She didn't beat him or burn him with cigarettes. She just, like, forgot she had a child. Some days she wouldn't feed him. Or change him. When she went out at night, she'd leave him all alone. Social workers asked questions, but there was no place else for him to go.

When Duncan was three, his grandfather died. "He was a total drunk. So was my mother, I think. I've got this fuzzy memory of broken bottles and a really bad smell. I'll never touch the stuff. Genetics, you know?"

"Is that when she joined the cult?" I asked. "After your grand-father died?"

Duncan covered his face. "There was no cult," he admitted, finally. "Nobody made her do anything. When I was three years old, she tracked down my father. He was living in a rented house in this crap neighborhood. She told me to go play in the back-yard. When I came back inside she was gone."

I stared at him. "She just left you?"

He nodded, and his nostrils flared a little. "My father didn't believe I was his kid. So she said she'd get the birth certificate out of her car, but instead she drove away."

"No cult," I reiterated. A cult actually made more sense.

He shook his head. "My dad asked me what my name was. But someone—maybe my mom, but I doubt it—once told me if a stranger asks you your name, don't tell them."

I ran a hand over his prickly hair and swallowed the lump in my throat. "What did your dad call you?"

"At first he called me Buddy. And then he said I could pick my own name."

"And you chose Duncan?"

He grinned. "Flash."

"*Flash?*"

"Yeah. But when I turned eight, I decided that maybe wasn't

so cool. So then I went through a bunch—Jake, Ricardo, Frankie, Dean—until I found one that felt right. I've been Duncan since I was twelve."

"Did you ever tell your dad your real name?"

"Oh, yeah. When I was five, my dad needed a birth certificate for school. The town where I'd been born only had one hospital, so it was pretty easy to track down. Then there was some more legal stuff my dad had to do to get official custody and change my last name to his, but it wasn't hard since my mother had deserted and no one else wanted me."

"Why didn't you just go back to Charles, then?"

His lips tightened. "It was the name she gave me. I didn't want anything from her."

I thought of Delilah's lost father. "Where's your mother now?"

He shrugged. "Don't know. Don't care."

"Not even a little?"

"No." He gazed off for a while, seeing something that wasn't there. "My dad's got his faults, but he would never leave me." He turned his head and looked me in the eye. "That's what I realized when I was on the island."

I shook my head in confusion.

"We landed, and I went around the shore and inland a bit because I had to . . . well, whatever. Anyway, afterward I started exploring, looking at the cliffs and plants and stuff, and I kinda lost track of time. And my dad came after me. I heard him calling out, and he sounded totally freaked. I mean, really terrified. I found him, and his face . . ." He bit his lip at the memory.

"What?"

212

"He was really pale and his eyes—it looked like he'd been crying. And he was all, 'Oh, my God, I didn't know where you were.' And that's when it hit me. If I tell him I want to stay here, he won't go off without me."

"You're staying," I whispered. "You're alive and you're staying."

He took his arm from around my shoulders and held my face in both of his hands. "There's something else. The other night . . . I thought about what you said, about helping me with my schoolwork. If you're still up for it—I'm in."

"You decided that . . . the night you walked me home?"

He flushed. "I felt like you were treating me like I was dumb, and it kind of pissed me off. But after I left you it suddenly hit me: 'Dude, don't be mad at her. It's totally your fault.' Like, maybe if I showed up to class, I might actually learn something."

I pictured Duncan's walk home from Home Suite Home: the dark street, the rustling trees, the tunnel under the highway. I pictured the fast-moving clouds and the night-light of a moon.

Relief bubbled up inside of me. "I'm not going to die!"

"Huh?"

"The camera! The pictures! They don't predict death at all. What's that thing Rose kept talking about? The transformational experience?"

He shook his head. "You lost me."

"Rose said that if we're lucky, we'll have transformational moments in our lives—realizations that change us forever. And during the transformation, a person sheds old energy. I think my camera captured that energy—just as if it were capturing light!"

213

"I still don't get it."

"Okay. First there was Francine Lunardi. We all knew she died. What we didn't know is that she'd just realized how much she'd loved her daughter. She'd finally managed to move beyond some bad stuff that happened years ago."

Duncan nodded.

"And then there was Ronald Young," I continued. "His wife came to see Rose yesterday. Turns out, as soon as he found out he was going to be a father, he became more responsible, more mature. Now you're telling me that you've decided to turn your life around. Don't you see? You'd all been transformed!"

Duncan stared at me.

"Am I starting to sound like Rose?" I asked.

"Worse."

"Well, maybe that's not such a bad thing." Okay, actually it was.

"But I don't get it," he said. "Why would you think you were going to die?" And then he understood. "Wait. You were in a photo?"

I popped off the couch and grabbed his hand. "I'll show you."

My dad was still on the patio. He turned and smiled. Wait till Duncan grew his hair back. There might not be so much smiling then.

"Hey, Dad, can I have my camera back?"

My dad's mouth and nose twitched. His face flushed. Something was wrong. "Yeah, um. Your camera. The thing is, that I, um . . ."

"What?"

"I dropped it," he admitted. "I was climbing up this rocky slope so I could get a picture of the building site. My feet slipped

214

and . . ." He sighed. "It's at the camera shop downtown. It's going to take a while to fix—three or four weeks."

I closed my eyes in irritation. "You made a psychic joke, didn't you?"

Duncan and I had almost made it to Psychic Photo when it hit me. "My clothes!"

He stopped and looked at my black shorts and black-and-pink-striped T-shirt. "I like what you're wearing. It's what you wore the first time I met you." He thought for a moment. "And also the second and third."

"No," I said. "My *good* clothes!"

When Duncan and I walked through the purple front door, Delilah beamed with pride. "I listed everything you gave me as a lot—you know, they'll all sell together for one price. Saves on shipping. You've had three bids already. You're up to twenty-nine dollars!"

"Oh, no!" I laid my head on the counter.

"Don't worry," Delilah said. "It's a seven-day auction. I bet it'll hit fifty bucks by the time it's over. Maybe more." Today Delilah wore a red sundress with white polka dots. Her dark hair was done up in two high pigtails. She looked like a punk Minnie Mouse.

"Do you know how much those clothes cost in the mall?" I asked.

She rolled her eyes. "Something ridiculous. I can't believe what people will pay when you can find the exact same thing at the thrift store for almost nothing. Remember how much great stuff I found last week?"

"Yeah, because *they were all my clothes*! Can we take the listing down?"

She shook her head. "Not once you've got bids. Didn't you want me to list them? I thought that's why you gave them to me."

"I did. It was. It's just—complicated." Delilah didn't know that I'd seen myself on the camera. I didn't feel quite ready to talk about it, to explain just how much I had changed. And anyway, changed or not, I still wanted my clothes. "Can I bid on the lot? And then just take the stuff back?"

Delilah considered. "You can set up a PayPal account if you've got a bank account or a credit card."

"So that would be a no."

She held her hands up in defeat. And then she remembered something. "I did save one thing out for you, though."

My Seven jeans? My board shorts? I was almost afraid to look, but when she held up the orange monstrosity I had to laugh. "My Dennis's Building Supply T-shirt. How did you know?"

She smiled. "I like it. It's got this whole hard-hat chic thing going on. I figured you'd be bummed if you sold it."

Maybe she wasn't psychic, after all.

Afterword

IN SEPTEMBER I STARTED MY SOPHOMORE YEAR at Sandyland High School. It's a regional school, which means there are kids bused in from all over. Like: from underground caves. And from jail. Okay, not really, but some of these kids are freaking scary, man, with dead eyes and greasy hair and, I swear to God, tattooed necks. They make Delilah look like she just walked out of Nordstrom.

Mostly, though, I still hang with Duncan and Delilah. And Leo, of course—who sold his disco ball for twenty-eight bucks on eBay (go figure) with an announcement that it's time to move on to the eighties. We're seeing a lot of neon and spandex these days and hoping the nineties are just around the corner.

After checking out the high school newspaper and declaring it lame beyond repair, Delilah and I launched an art-and-literary magazine called *Flash*. (That was Duncan's suggestion.) We let everyone interested join the staff because we wanted to be inclusive. Well, and also because there were only three other people who signed up, one of whom was Duncan, who mostly comes for the snacks.

Duncan has made remarkable progress. He is reading at an eleventh-grade level, studying calculus, and learning Latin.

Ha! As if. But after, like, twenty hours of intensive practice, I think he finally knows how to use quotation marks. At least, most of the time. When he thinks about it. Next we are going to tackle apostrophes. I can hardly wait.

Truth is, we both get frustrated sometimes. Often. Almost all of the time. But there are moments of triumph and I know it's all been worthwhile. Last week he took a test on periods (not that kind of period), and he got everything right. I was so proud of him that I photocopied the test at the grocery store (as an employee's daughter I pay . . . full price), and then we both taped it to our refrigerators.

Yes, we have a refrigerator now: full-size. There's also a real stove and oven—not that my mother knows how to use them, but at least the possibility exists. Most days she looks pretty tired, and I hate to say it, but she looks older than she did when we lived in Amerige. But she gets up every day and she goes to work, and then she comes home to her family. It's not a perfect life, but it's a life.

And by the way, I was totally right about her decorating the cottage with flowered curtains and shabby-chic furniture.

My dad's looking better than he has in years, if only because he's outside all day getting sun and exercise. Plus, he's trying to save money by bringing his lunch, which he packs in a cooler the size of New Jersey. My mom gives him bagged salad and deli items that have passed their sell-by date—which is exactly what I will tell the emergency room doctors on the inevitable day when he is rushed in with food poisoning.

After Rose's mini-breakdown when she thought Larry was dead (don't blame me; I was just using the information I had available at the time), we all thought they'd get married, but they haven't. The weird thing is, now it's Rose who's doing all kinds of nice things for Larry and begging him to commit. He does nice things back—I think he can't help himself—but he wants to make sure she's in it for the long run. Or maybe he just wants to focus his energies on Duncan. Or maybe he just likes hearing her beg. Can you blame him?

About a month after we moved into the little yellow house (which my mother, no joke, has taken to calling "The Rose Cottage"), Lexie came for a weekend. It was weird. When she got off the train, my first thought wasn't about how much I've missed her or about how nervous I was, but: *I wish I had her shirt.* It was pale blue with a picture of a pink pig with white wings.

I said, "I like your shirt."

She said, "It's from Glamour Kills. I had to order it online because they didn't have it at the mall."

And you'd think I'd be above it all by now after my big transformation, that I'd realize that shirts don't matter, but this emptiness shot through me that I recognized as *want*. It's a nasty feeling, and it hits me more than I'd like. Maybe my transformation wasn't complete—or maybe we never truly shed our old selves but just uncover the better parts that were there all along.

Lexie and I met up with Duncan, Delilah, and Leo at the beach. Though it was starting to grow out, Duncan's hair was still shortish, which made his new skull earrings (seventy-five cents at a yard sale) that much easier to see. I flushed with embarrassment at my freaky boyfriend—and then I flushed with shame at my embarrassment. Delilah's and Leo's clothes were relatively normal, but Delilah was sporting a fresh magenta streak in her hair, while Leo's bright orange locks had been gelled and blown like an eighties pop star's.

Later that night, after Lexie had changed into a soft white camisole and flowered boxer shorts while I put on—shoot me now—my Dennis's Building Supply T-shirt, she said, "I like your friends." She didn't meet my eyes.

"Yeah, they're nice," I said, hoping that was all we needed to say on the subject. We'd already spent a good two hours talking about Rolf (who—surprise!—was turning out to be a wiener), but I thought we could get a little more mileage out of Celia.

"They're . . . different from our friends at home."

"Mmm," I said, thinking—those aren't "our" friends anymore.

She sighed sadly. "They're so much more *interesting*."

I put my arms around her. We hugged and had a good girl-cry. I said, "You'll always be my best friend." And she said, "You'll always be my best friend, too." And we both meant it in some way, even as we both knew it wasn't true.

After Lexie left, I found the flying pig T-shirt with a note that said, "For my BFF." But I couldn't take Lexie's charity, so I put the shirt in a padded envelope and sent it back to her.

Oh. My. God. Please tell me you didn't fall for that. Of course I kept it! It looks fabulous on me.

My camera didn't take three or four weeks to fix. Larry had it back to me the next day, along with a new memory card. He said the old one was fried, the shots all gone. At first I was upset about losing the memory card because I'd wanted to print the

220

pictures of Duncan and me, but I got over it. Sometimes you have to move on.

My camera still goes everywhere with me. Delilah lets me download my pictures onto her computer, and we study the shots together. In the fall, when there's hardly ever any fog, Sandyland's light is so clear it's almost magical.

Nothing strange has turned up since my camera spent another night at Psychic Photo. I'm okay with that.

I'll leave you with a final snapshot.

I stand at the ocean's edge in the late afternoon, the colors deep and the shadows strong. The foamy water rolls in, ready to splash, and—*snap!* I catch the very instant when the sea touches my toes, as dry becomes wet and warm becomes cold.

But we all know that time doesn't stop like that. It's just a photo, after all.

Acknowledgments

A million thanks to my editor, Farrin Jacobs, for her extreme patience and brilliant insights—and also for working weekends to produce those five-page (single-spaced) revision letters. Farrin, I'd say, "I couldn't have done it without you"—but surely you know that by now.

Thanks, too, to Gretchen Hirsch for her valuable input; Kari Sutherland for handling so many details, big and small; Melissa Bruno for "spreading the word"; and Sasha Illingworth for the wonderfully spooky cover.

As always, I am grateful to my agent, Stephanie Kip Rostan, for her competence, intelligence, and humor; and to Monika Verma, Miek Coccia, Elizabeth Bishop, Melissa Rowland, and the rest of the Levine Greenberg team for taking care of so many details so I can just write. And play with my cats. But mostly write.

Finally, thanks to my family for giving me the space and time to build a world filled with my imaginary friends. I love you more than them. Really.